MIST

THE FIRST TAVISTOCK ALLAN MYSTERY

MIST

The First Tavistock Allan Mystery

by

Linda Mann

The Pentland Press Limited
Edinburgh · Cambridge · Durham · USA

© Linda Mann 2001

First published in 2001 by
The Pentland Press Ltd.
1 Hutton Close
South Church
Bishop Auckland
Durham

All rights reserved.
Unauthorised duplication
contravenes existing laws.

British Library Cataloguing in Publication Data.
A catalogue record for this book is available
from the British Library.

ISBN 1 85821 828 4

Typeset by George Wishart & Associates, Whitley Bay.
Printed and bound by Antony Rowe Ltd., Chippenham.

*To my parents, John and Sylvia with love
and
to my friend Sandie for her unfailing honesty*

Although this book is set in and around the Isle of Man, a real island lounging in the middle of the Irish Sea, all other characters and some of the places are purely fictitious and any similarity to anybody living or dead is simply coincidence and the product of my overworked imagination.

In the Beginning

I have lived a long, long time; sometimes, I admit, it feels too long. My home for over two thousand years has been an Island, thirty-two miles long and thirteen miles wide, a place of mountains, glens and sandy bays, of cliffs and grey ragged skies. My people and I still fondly think of the inhabitants in this way, who have governed themselves for over a thousand years. They have their own language and currency and pride and because of this still live in safety amongst themselves and others.

I used to be known as Mannanan Mac Lir, navigator and magician and some say God of this small piece of ancient rock. I could call up a hundred men out of the mists to frighten my enemies and when I laid my cloak against the ground the Island and all its quivering souls would vanish. However, that was long ago when the Celts and Druids worshipped the elements, before the Viking longboats beached upon sandy inlets. They arrived and then settled because my power had been forfeit many years before to the Irish Christians and their Saints. It was a way of staying here in early retirement, the offer of life in legend, a far cry from the complete abandonment of other Gods, as happened across the waters. So I have lived on, remembered but not venerated. It has been a fairly easy existence. I keep the ley lines open and cleaned; my cloak is spread over the high peaks every June and August if only to keep the grating wasp-like sound of motor bikes from becoming too encroaching. Mind you, people remember me then and for a while I become, almost, alive.

It was yesterday that I walked with the sheep amongst the grey-green wind-twisted trees of Druidale. Soft rain fell and as I walked I thought I smelt fresh human blood. The awakening sun glowed weakly just above the hills and when I looked to the ancient wooded stream I could see a naked figure smeared rust brown. It tittered and danced and finally sank exhausted to the ground. I saw it smile as if remembering the feel of warm flesh, the victim's eyes glazed with pain and terror. Death glinted on each cut made by the great curved blade it lovingly held in both hands.

Above, a body hung by its ankles, the gaping wound where a neck used to be livid against the grey whiteness of the skin and tangled mane of dark hair. It swung gently in the breeze. The ropes emitted faint echoes of the scream which had stopped abruptly as the vocal cords had finally severed.

It was then that I swore in the ancient tongue of the Tuatha De Danann and I spat twice upon the ground; then I spread my cloak against the trees to hide this outrage against my people and my pact with the Holy Saint, Patrick.

I sit here now, beside the cold steel columns built upon my beloved mountain Snaefell and sorrow sits with me. A killer walks amongst my children. I looked into its eyes and know that unless I can somehow touch someone of today and stop the madness, it will kill again and again and again.

1st April

George Allan rushed through the back door and after stuffing the last piece of buttered toast into his mouth announced,

'There's a body in a bin bag in the fish pond and it smells.'

Tavistock Allan, who was trying to feed the cat, start the washing machine and deal with the waste disposal from hell, muttered, 'Yes, dear,' and pushed another couple of slices of bread into the toaster. It was April the first and so far her husband Richard had blackened his face with the soap carefully left in the shower by his eldest daughter Kate. She had already been fooled by the plastic dog poo left on the kitchen floor, even though they didn't have a dog. So a body in a bin bag for a writer of detective thrillers was not going to be taken too seriously, although she had to admit that it did beat the severed hand, made of jelly, she'd found in the fridge the previous year.

George watched carefully for signs of intelligent life and finding none, sighed as only the average six-year-old can when afflicted with a particularly stupid parent.

'It's a big black bin bag and it really smells, Mum, worse than that dead rabbit Captain Pugwash caught and left in the coal bunker. That time when we went to Lanzarote to stay with Grandpa and the lid fell down and Daddy didn't find it for weeks and when he did there was maggots everywhere and Uncle James used them for bait and caught the really big trout Grandpa had been after for years.' At last he took in great gulps of air. 'Remember, Mum? I'm telling the truth; it's not a wind up. Honest it's not.'

George watched the words sink in and in desperation tugged at his mother's sleeve.

'Is anybody in there?' he shouted.

'George, don't be rude to your mother, you know she's not a morning person.'

MIST

His father, who had just entered the kitchen, glared at his eldest daughter whilst still trying to remove the last of the black stain from his face. Carefully he opened the fridge door and peered inside. Visibly sighing with relief he pulled out a fresh carton of milk and grabbed a box of cereal from the kitchen table. There was a watchful silence as he carefully poured rice crispies and black plastic spiders into his bowl.

'George says there's a body in the fishpond, Dad; mind you, he also said Grandma was a World War Two spy and then went and worked in the same newspaper office as Superman!' uttered Kate with all the superiority of an eight-year-old, putting younger brother well in his place.

'Grandma as Mata Hari! The mind boggles.'

'Richard!' Tavistock growled, scraping chocolate spread off the overloaded slice her youngest had been in the process of demolishing. 'You, madam, will have no teeth left,' she admonished. 'And did you do that?' she added, pointing to her husband who was carefully fishing spiders out of his cereal bowl with a fork.

Nobody answered except George, who was now making loud snorting noises of frustration.

Richard Allan looked up from his excavations and saw that his son's whole body was trembling with angry indignation. Some intuition told him that George wasn't joking this time and however unlikely, it was worth investigation, especially as the idea of breakfast had palled somewhat. Spiders he could take with a certain amount of equanimity but the lifelike millipede in the sugar bowl was something else. So before war could be declared between siblings he announced in loud tones that he would investigate the pond immediately. Escorted by his offspring, including the four-year-old still clutching the now soggy bread, chocolate dribbling down her chin, his darkly muttering spouse and the cat, Richard Allan marched off down the garden towards the pond.

Detective Inspector Callow wasn't in the best of moods. The morning had not started well at all and after tasting the coffee from

MIST

the latest in coffee-killing machines, yet another wise cost-cutting exercise beloved by the bureaucrats in Tynwald, it wasn't getting any better. The phone rang somewhere under the pile of papers, newly delivered by a sweating PC.

'Yes!' he barked whilst desperately trying to find the chocolate biscuits he'd secreted somewhere in his desk.

'It's Tavistock Allan for you, Sir.'

'Who?' The biscuits were being particularly elusive, in fact so much so that he was beginning to wonder if the buggers on nights had found them.

'The lady writer, you know the one that writes all them crime novels with modern women with brains and no tits.'

'Oh, yes. Em, what does she want then, more advice on the drugs squad and how to catch yo-yo smugglers? Ah, got you!'

'Sir?' The puzzled voice on the end of the line was then the recipient of some very strange shuffling and fumbling noises ending in a primal scream of unholy glee, cut very short on the discovery of one treble wrapped chocolate digestive.

'Well, come on, lad, spit it out, some of us have work to do and people to see.'

'She says she's found a body in a bin bag in her ornamental fishpond and would we come round and take it away. I'll put her through now, shall I, Sir?' and without waiting for a reply the line went quiet and Tavistock Allan found herself passed along the line, for the fifth time but not in as many minutes.

'Bob, is that you?' Tavistock was beginning to wish that she'd taken her son's advice and done a proper Viking funeral with a large quantity of lighter fuel and several bags of barbecue briquettes. It would have been quicker than trying to track down Robert Callow on the morning of April the first, especially when everyone knew what you did for a living.

'Ah, Tavistock. I, er, hear you have a body in your fishpond. This isn't the usual Manx Radio wind up, or bad taste prank perpetrated by my overimaginative godson, is it? Because if it is, somebody, somewhere, will seriously rue his birthday! And young George may not live to see his!'

'No, Bob, it unfortunately isn't. There is a putrefying body, complete with assorted stages of blowfly, in a black bin bag in my fishpond. The builders are due at any moment to start on the roof, Richard is still being sick in the downstairs loo and if someone doesn't take me seriously I shall personally sue the lot of you!'

Bob Callow sighed. If Tavistock was considering coughing up legal fees to a bunch of overpaid smartarse advocates then this was real and a day which had started in first gear if not reverse was about to go into overdrive.

'I'll be right over. And Tavistock, please, don't touch anything.'

The line went dead. Tavistock switched the mobile off and looked down on the black wrapped object grotesquely floating amongst the carrot coloured fish and dark green weed.

'I wasn't going to,' she muttered angrily as she turned and headed off down the drive to open the gate.

Tavistock sat in her mock Tudor kitchen and hugged the large mud-coloured coffee mug to her, as if to ward off demons or at the very least the shabby figure of Bob Callow, who had managed to scrounge not only four large mugs of tea off her but had also found the tin of Festive Assorted biscuits which she'd hidden from the children at Christmas and had lost up to now.

'Bob, how long before they, er, know anything?'

'The pathologist? God knows. How long's a piece of string? Did you know you had three types of chocolate creams in here?'

Tavistock sighed. It had been a long morning. George had thrown a major temper tantrum and refused to leave the scene of the crime until a kindly WPC, who had children of her own, had offered to run him to school in a proper police car. She said it was on her way to police headquarters anyway and although that comment was met with a raised eyebrow or two, the thought of no George and no questions, which were coming like machine gun bullets at millisecond intervals, swung it. So George and his sisters had been driven to school in style. The builders had spent most of the morning sitting in the scaffolding alternately drinking tea, scratching and smoking, like a large denim clad flock of vultures, whilst the roof still leaked.

Richard had eventually been allowed to leave for the office, grey faced and thin-lipped. Tavistock couldn't decide whether it had been the shock of finding the body or discovering that his son and heir had inherited his mother's morbid taste for death. Either way things were certain to be strained upon his return to what he had bitingly referred to as the family morgue. Within minutes of his departure her publisher had rung to ask whether she could just have another look at the ending of chapter four again and the American style foil jacket she had hated on sight was the one the publicity department had finally opted for.

All in all, the day couldn't sink much lower: that was until the arrival of a breathless PC who stammered his way through a long and involved speech, which proved, eventually, to be the information that a man walking his dog had come upon something pretty odd near the stream at the old abandoned farm in Druidale. Tavistock sighed with relief: finally she would be left in peace to type, wash and defrost, a hope short lived.

'Er, I, em, don't suppose you could give me a lift, could you, love?' Bob tried to look pathetic but only managed vaguely seedy. 'Only the WPC took my car and hasn't come back yet; besides, think of it as a sort of hands-on workshop; at least then you can get the scene of crime bits right in those daft books of yours.'

Tavistock bit back a fairly acid reply and the phone above the fridge rang again. It could be my editor, she thought. 'OK, you win, Bob. If today is going to be useless as far as the great novel goes, it might as well be completely useless, and no comments about rally drivers or death on the roads or you'll be walking from Kate's Cottage!'

Tavistock parked as near to the long skeins of white and red plastic tape as she could and the car, a long pod-like people-carrier, sank gently into about six inches of churned mud and gravel.

'Oh, shit! That's it, the last straw, I'm going back to bed and I'm staying there until the next rotten New Year rears its ugly little head.'

MIST

'I'd come with you, love, but Moira would object,' Bob muttered, eyeing the mud outside and his almost new shoes inside, in almost the same glance.

'I don't suppose you could see your way to . . . ' Bob stole a quick look at Tavistock's frosty profile complete with clenched teeth, and sighed. Now was most definitely not the time to ask whether she would move the car. 'Ah well, I'd better go and see what it is that has made so many busy folks even busier. Want to have a look? No, never mind, eh. Anyway, thanks for the lift. I'll scrounge a ride back with Brian there.'

Bob opened the door and jumped as far as he could away from the sodden roadside and neatly landed on one of the largest heaps of sheep turds he had ever seen. He then proceeded to dance his way towards the clutch of constables sheltering from the steadily dripping rain, within the ruined walls and partially roofed remains of an old Manx farmhouse.

'Haven't you lot got anything better to do than to laugh at a superior officer?' he growled, grimly wiping the greeny-black remains from his shoes with a bunch of coarse grass and an old piece of slate he'd found by the doorway.

'No Sir, I mean yes Sir, only they won't let us touch anything until the scene of crime wizards have bagged everything that isn't a couple of metres down and bedrock, Sir.' Having thus informed his superior as to the status quo, Brian Clague fished in his pocket for a soggy cigarette and even wetter matches and spent the next five minutes trying to coax either, or both, of them to light, preferably at the same time.

Bob watched as nylon coated aliens photographed, brushed and picked about around the old knurled trees nearest the road and the stream. They seemed very interested in one particular tree. Curiosity being one of his strongest traits, Bob sauntered over towards the area of most activity, carefully eyeing the ground with every step. It was only as he neared the tree and looked up that he saw the white corpse swaying in the gentle breeze and it was then he realised that something had arrived on the Island that he was almost totally incapable of dealing with.

MIST

He stood below the tree, careful to disturb nothing, in the full and certain knowledge that if he did the Chief Constable would give him at least an hour of carefully vented fury, on 'how to muck up the evidence'! As the cold began to seep slowly through his coat so too did the horror of his find. Inwardly shuddering, he turned from the corpse and looked around him.

'Right then, Bob lad, pull yourself together.' He thought to himself. 'First things first, let's just have a look around and see if we can see some other poor sod who knows more than I do, and let's hope to God it's not a policeman.'

Squinting into the mist and struggling sunshine, Bob suddenly spotted a small brownish figure squatting precariously upon an old log and he looked, Bob realised to his delight, as if he were writing.

'Seth Riley!' Bob shouted, causing Seth to sit up so suddenly that the log tipped and he slid to the ground, narrowly avoiding the second largest heap of sheep turds.

'Bugger!' exclaimed Seth.

'Sorry about that, Seth. I was just so pleased to see someone I might get some half decent information from.' As Bob continued to apologise Seth picked himself up and began to collect notebook and pencils from where they had fallen amongst the long strands of couch grass and weeds.

'Well, don't think you're going to get anything from me. You can read my report like everyone else!'

'Ah, come on, Seth. There's no need to be like that. Look, how about if I buy you a pie and a pint on the way back and I'll even throw in a pudding too. Can't say fairer than that now, can I?'

Seth wiped one of the pencils and after inspecting its shiny silver exterior for the slightest sign of anything even vaguely biological, began to chew it thoughtfully. He had a very sweet tooth and his wife had recently insisted he eat only low fat healthy and extremely boring puddings, mostly containing yoghurt and usually foreign yoghurt at that.

'Well,' said Seth, visibly weakening. 'If it's a golden syrup steamed roll with double custard, I might feel free to discuss the matter more fully. Pull up a log.'

'Pretty grim, eh?' Bob muttered pointing upwards to the body which was now being lowered to the ground by at least three plastic-coated figures.

Seth continued to chew thoughtfully. 'Actually, what I'd like to know is, who would go to the trouble of climbing all the way up there just to cut a throat, to say nothing of tying him by his ankles first. Before you ask, the deceased climbed up too. He was alive, you see, before the throat cutting got going. No sign of a struggle though; odd, very odd.'

Seth spat bits of wood and graphite onto the ground.

'How do you make that out? The co-operation of the victim, I mean. Oh shit, you mean you went up there!' Bob viewed his friend with new-found respect and suddenly felt a very powerful craving for the cigarettes he'd recently given up.

'Sod that for a game of soldiers!' Bob dug his hands further into his coat pocket and shivered.

'Them buggers,' Seth waved his hands in the general direction of the stooping aliens, 'wanted me to certify that the poor sod was dead. I mean, there he is hanging from a bloody great tree, naked as the day he was born, with his throat almost cut out and not a drop of the old haemoglobin in him, and they want me to certify he's dead. Sometimes I seriously wonder about the state of education on this poor benighted rock!' Seth spat again and sighed.

Bob watched in morbid fascination as yet more photographs were taken, until finally the body was zipped, almost lovingly, into the matt black bodybag.

'So who did it then? The butler?'

Bob clenched his teeth and counted to five under his breath before turning round.

'Sod you, Tavistock, so help me, if you come up behind me again like that I'll do you for loitering and parking in a restricted area!'

'Ah well, that's why I'm still here. Any chance some of your lot who aren't actually doing anything, which by the way is most of them, would throw a couple of shovel loads of gravel under the car's wheels? So I can go home and leave you in peace.'

'That's not a car, it's a bus, especially the way you drive it! Although strictly speaking, I suppose, it's not absolutely necessary to have all four wheels on the ground, at the same time.' Tavistock glared back at him. 'All right, all right, I'll see what I can do. Just don't touch anything. Oh, and by the way, you can use the log if you like, it's still warm.'

Bob chuckled in a manner which would have had most feminists reaching for a sharp kitchen knife and stalked off to find the nearest, wettest Police Constable.

'Morning, Tavistock. How are the kids? Little Emily's sore throat clear up all right? Nasty virus that!'

'Yes, thanks and the others are fine or they were until this morning when George found a body in the fishpond.' Tavistock sighed and tried to find a more comfortable bit of warmed log.

'George would! By the way, as you're here, would you mind telling me why you described me as a bearded old gnome in your last book? Know what I got as a fiftieth birthday surprise? No, not a nubile young nurse dying to take her clothes off whilst singing "Happy Birthday to You", but a bloody great bamboo pole with a plastic fish on the end and one of the scariest woolly hats you've ever seen!'

'Oh.'

'Well may you say, "oh", young lady. Very nearly sent you an appropriate letter with an advocate's signature at the bottom!'

'Don't suppose you'd like a mint imperial?' Tavistock produced a small white paper bag from the inside pocket of her coat and smiled ingratiatingly.

'Hmm, all right but next time less of the "old" if you don't mind. The gnome bit, fair enough, but old, that's just plain nasty!'

Seth slowly sucked on his mint and his thoughts began to turn towards the word 'Lunch', preferably large and more importantly, free! Tavistock, who was saving up memories of a real crime scene for the next book, realised with a start that she could see a man leaning against a leafless tree. He was almost out of sight but she could have sworn that he had been staring back at her. Something tugged in her brain somewhere, an old memory long buried.

'Seth.'

'Umm.'

'Who is that old man?'

'What old man?'

'That old man, over there by the elm.' Tavistock pointed in the direction of the tree and Seth peered through dampened lenses, trying to pick the old man out.

'Can't see anything at all; mind you, I don't like the look of that sheep at all. Now there's the face of a true psychopath, if ever I saw one!'

'What are you both looking at?' asked Bob. For a fairly stolid man he could move with almost feline stealth; unfortunately it was only when totally sober.

'I really do wish you wouldn't creep up on people like that,' muttered Seth, standing up and collecting his belongings. 'Tavistock thinks she's seen an old man watching her from those trees, the ones near the rabid sheep.'

'Oh, him. He's been sneaking around all morning. I've told the lads to see him off when they catch him. Bloody ghouls!'

'Do you think he might have seen something?' asked Tavistock, who had the oddest feeling she ought to know the man but couldn't for the life of her remember why.

'Shouldn't think so, love. He more than likely came down to see whether we were making another of them films or something. One of the lads said they filmed a bit of "Waking Ned" here. He's been moonlighting as an extra, would you believe! I told him, you just wait till I tell the boss, bringing the Force into disrepute, especially with a face like yours. You know what he said?'

Tavistock and Seth shook their heads.

'He said it was community policing! Cheeky bastard! Right, well, the bus is now free to go, how about joining us for a pie and a pint? You can drive.'

Bob grinned, a grin cut short by Seth who declared, 'Join us by all means. Uncle Bob's kindly offered to pay and there's pudding!'

'Not golden syrup with double custard?'

'The very same.'

'Well in that case it would be churlish to refuse and you can both fill me in on all the gory details!'

Tavistock and Seth picked their way back to the car. Bob followed more slowly busily intent on investigating various zipped pockets for loose change. Finally he found two fives, a quantity of ten pence pieces and a screwed up twenty-pound note he didn't even know he had. Sighing with relief he almost ran after the two retreating figures, unaware that the old man was walking almost directly behind him.

Tavistock poured the remaining bubble bath into the blue foaming water and slid gratefully down into the hot froth. After her limbs began to feel almost young, she reached for the double malt on the side of the bath and opened her book at the turned over edge. It was the latest Rankin and she had been looking forward to this moment ever since she had picked up her warring offspring from school. How, she wondered, could three fairly intelligent children possibly start a full-scale war simply because one of them had looked at the other one? Tea had been greeted with the words 'But I don't like casserole!' from George who had spent the previous teatime bemoaning the fact that she never cooked him anything he liked, like casserole. Tavistock had held her breath and offered to cook him if he didn't eat it! Then Emily had dropped yoghurt and blackcurrants down herself, the chair, the floor and the cat who had been sitting under the table in the mistaken belief that he would be safe there. Kate had her bath and five minutes before bedtime announced that she was going to the House of Mannanan with the school and could she have a packed lunch and would Mummy mind getting her to school before ten to nine so she could catch the bus. Mummy did mind. The bread was still in the freezer and she hadn't yet been to the shops. Richard then rang to say he was delayed and would be home by about nine thirty, totally forgetting that they were supposed to be going out to dinner with her parents. It had been a very long day, so much so that when someone said, 'Excuse me for barging in but would it be possible to have a quiet word?' she assumed it was

Richard back early and laden with guilt preferably in the form of wine or chocolates.

It then dawned on her that the bathroom door was bolted on the inside and her spine tingled unpleasantly as she felt prickles of adrenaline. Without wanting to and beginning to realise that Stephen King was vastly underrated, she turned her head towards the voice, willing herself to open her eyes and look.

Time seemed to stop, for what she saw was a shadowy figure of an old man wearing what looked like a brown dressing gown, sitting on the toilet. He was smiling.

'Who the hell are you?' hissed Tavistock.

'Mannanan Mac Lir, at your service.' The figure stood up, sketched a remarkably graceful bow and sat down again.

'Mannanan? But you're a god, or a ghost or folklore or something. Hang on, Kate did a project on you last term. You must be a malt whisky. You can't possibly be here in my bathroom, and certainly not sitting, well, where you're sitting.' Tavistock eyed the remaining amber fluid with a certain degree of suspicion but drank it all anyway.

'I prefer to be thought of as a spirit or very elderly resident. This is a very lovely bathroom by the way; I've always liked blue and gold and it's warm. Yes, there are distinct possibilities with this room.'

'You're not staying here, I don't care who you are! This is the only room with a door I can lock. Go and inspect the spare room or how about the lounge; the fire's lit in there?'

'Right, well, I'll go then. Perhaps we could talk later when you have some clothes on or even not. It's been a long time since I've seen a naked woman, alive that is; makes a nice change, I must say.'

Tavistock reached over to the towel rail and swore as her book sank under the water. Mannanan moved towards her. The book suddenly flew from the water, shook itself terrier-like and flapped in mid air. Tavistock screamed and Mannanan Mac Lir merged with the upwardly swirling steam and disappeared.

Later, in bed with Richard, Tavistock asked gently whether he believed in ghosts. Richard, half asleep, assured her that there really was no such thing.

'Well, in that case,' thought his wife to herself, 'there really isn't anyone sitting in the window seat with his feet on the radiator.'

7th April

Bob sat on a wooden bench in St. George's churchyard. The seat he'd chosen was the one just to the side of the memorial to Sir William Hillary and behind the cholera pit. To be honest, his first thoughts on hearing about this particular meeting place were not complimentary but now that he was here, he was positively enjoying the warm April sunshine. Birds sang noisily in the big sycamores flanking the church wall and the first insects buzzed around the flowers and weeds growing between the cool grey stones.

He was teetering on the verge of sleep when he felt someone blow in his ear, so he closed his eyes tighter and pretended he hadn't felt a thing.

'You're no fun any more, Bob Callow. The least you could do is jump!' muttered Tavistock, settling down on the other end of the bench. She had a large canvas bag with her, which she began to rifle through.

'This is, I must admit, rather pleasant. In fact, I was even beginning to wish I'd brought some sandwiches and a flask of coffee with me.' Bob sighed and wriggled his toes.

'Well it's just as well I did then.' Tavistock placed a foil wrapped package on the bench between them and began to pour out hot milky coffee into two plastic mugs.

Bob opened his eyes and started carefully to unwrap the foil-square, gleefully discovering large doorstops of cheese and tomato.

'How did you know? These are my favourite sarnies.' Bob bit deep and discovered they also contained liberal amounts of salad cream. Tavistock watched, trying to gauge how the secret ingredient beloved by all her offspring and now included in all sandwiches out of habit more than anything, would go down in the adult world.

'My Dad used to make doorstops like these. Can I have another?'

'Please do. I've got some cake as well, for afters.'

Tavistock and Bob munched in companionable silence.

'So then, where's this man of yours?' Bob asked, scooping milky skin off the top of his coffee with his finger.

'In the library looking something up. It's only round the corner so he shouldn't be too long.'

A car drew into the churchyard and parked beside the tower wall. After a few minutes a figure got out clutching a collection of files, waved to them and walked back down the drive towards the main gates.

'Who's that, then?' asked Bob, wiping a large blob of salad cream from his chin with a not overly clean, large white cotton handkerchief.

'The Archdeacon.'

'Oh.'

As the Archdeacon neared the gates another man somewhat older in appearance entered the churchyard and walked straight through him. The vicar walked on unconcerned and Bob dropped his coffee.

'Bloody Hell!'

'You really should stop swearing, Bob Callow, especially here. This is consecrated ground, you know. Good morning, Tavistock. Mind if I join you?'

The elderly man sat between them on the bench and began to massage his knees through the soft folds of cloth covering them. Bob remained speechlessly staring at him while Tavistock, with a total lack of concern which Bob found even more unnerving, began to hand round rectangles of fruit cake.

'You just, that is . . . you couldn't have, could you?' Bob heard himself gibbering. Pull yourself together man, he told himself.

'Yes, please do, then we can get down to discussing these murders sensibly and yes, I can read thoughts, especially when the mind is as easily read as yours.' Mannanan Mac Lir smiled kindly, although a trifle myopically, at Bob and rubbed his eyes with the sleeve of his gown.

'Tavistock, please tell me that your idea of a good snout is not someone who's very obviously dead!'

MIST

'Bob, will you just calm down a minute. This gentleman is Mannanan Mac Lir, navigator, magician and, er, minor venerated person and, despite the fact that he just also happens to be of the spirit world, has some information for you. So please just put disbelief to one side and listen. After all, it's not as if you have a huge number of leads, is it!'

'I don't have any,' Bob muttered, reaching for the flask and pouring himself some more coffee.

'Right, so you definitely need to listen. Have another piece of cake.' Tavistock handed him a large slab of rich fruitcake and as he ate Mannanan talked.

'I suppose you would like to know why you can see me and others can't?' Bob nodded. He'd already come to the uncomfortable conclusion that this was the old man he'd clearly seen at Druidale, the one that he'd had every available constable looking for, fruitlessly, for the rest of the day.

'In this lady's case it is because she has inherited "The Sight" from her great, great grandmother, who was reputed to have been a witch. In fact the whole thing can probably be explained by anyone interested in ESP or telepathy. Tavistock sees things with the subconscious but instead of burying it, allows the brain to view the image as normal. At least, I believe that's how it works, or as near as I can make out. You see, I frequently go to the library. They have a very good paranormal section and it's warm. Just in case you're wondering how an old so and so like myself can possibly have a modern opinion on anything.' Bob grinned and bowed his head in acknowledgement.' As for you, young Callow, the reason you see me is much more straightforward. You have a genetic memory passed down through the ages.'

'Genetic memory?'

'I slept with your great, great, great etc grandmother.'

Bob opened his mouth to speak, couldn't, and realised to his surprise that it did make a kind of sense, albeit not the kind he'd willingly repeat to a superior officer.

'Unfortunately, although I did see your murderer, I didn't actually see him or at least not the way you would.'

'How do you mean?' Bob asked.

'Well, everybody has several sides to their personality. For instance, the way we perceive how we look is not necessarily how we are seen by other people.'

Bob nodded; the concept wasn't new but he was beginning to wonder where Mannanan was going with it.

'The best way I can explain all this is that as a Spirit I tend to see reality in a more spiritual fashion. In other words you see through your eyes and I see through my senses or my soul, for want of a more technical term. This murderer of yours is someone that has two very different faces: the one he wears every day, the trusted loved face, and the one he wears when he kills. When I looked at him the two were blurred so that I couldn't actually physically see him. And even if I described him accurately it would be of very little help and I doubt whether if drawn it would look any different than a hallowe'en mask of the Devil or average medieval gargoyle.'

'Oh,' Bob said.

'I can, however pick up emotions and thoughts from him, but only when he is in the act of killing or whenever his everyday mask is lowered.'

'You mean, you can't tell us what this nutter looks like but you can tell us why he might have done it?' said Bob, still trying to come to terms with the fact that he was talking to a dead person and that said dead person was the only witness to a crime he was desperate to solve.

'Well no, not exactly, although I can tell you how he felt while he was doing it but the why, I think you will have to go back to the past for that. He was born here, I would say maybe nearly forty years ago, left for a considerable length of time and has now returned. I felt as I watched him dance that he was here for a very specific purpose and that there is nothing random about these killings.'

Bob sighed. The last week had been fraught with reporters asking questions no one could answer, followed by politicians asking questions no one wanted to answer. The Minister for Tourism, who was terrified that the murders would curtail an already short tourist

MIST

season and in particular frighten off tourists coming over for the TT, had had a particularly vitriolic meeting with the Chief Constable. The Chief Constable had then personally relayed the ministerial message down the command chain, adding a few choice words of his own. And now it looked like the only lead he had was going to assist him to the local funny farm, even quicker than his small band of detective constables could hope for.

'There is one thing I can tell you, though.'

'Yes,' Bob cried, almost too eagerly. This was it. Case solved, back to shoplifting and the odd burnt-out car.

'He will kill again, unless you can stop him.'

'Why am I not surprised!' muttered Bob despairingly.

'You see, he enjoys it too much to stop.' Mannanan sighed wearily. 'I think maybe you ought to look at the background of both victims, especially the one young George found.'

'Look, I know they're connected; I just don't know how or even why.' Bob sat back with arms folded and his best 'So tell me something I don't know' expression fixed to his features.

'Bob, just how many murders do you usually have?'

'About two or three a year, mostly domestic or drugs,' Bob admitted thoughtfully.

'So resources are not exactly stretched? I know this creature killed both of them and he had a reason for doing it; go through everything again, as soon as you have the identities of the two victims.'

'I presume you're not trying to teach me my job?' Bob muttered morosely.

'Wouldn't dream of it.' Mannanan looked out over the graveyard and sighed. 'It isn't often that you come across something that is almost pure evil; most people have some redeeming quality. I remember watching a play by that young chap who came over in sixteen something or other. One of the main characters was almost a study in deceit and death; the only redeeming feature he had was that his wife loved him. Now what was his name?'

'Iago. Nasty piece of work.' Bob saw Tavistock's look of surprise and frowned. 'Saw *Othello* at Stratford with Moira the other year.

MIST

Just because I'm a copper doesn't mean to say I don't do anything else. I dunno, you writers seem to think you have first dibs on anything artistic and that the rest of the world are either related to sheep or are totally brain dead.'

'Bob, put the chip away. The reason I showed surprise was that I hadn't realised Shakespeare even knew where the Isle of Man was, let alone stayed here,' Tavistock replied.

Mannanan, taking no notice of either, rambled on. 'That's the one, showed a lot of promise but was always broke. The poor chap had absolutely no idea how to budget. The ladies loved him. I remember we had a few nice chats. He actually said he'd put me in one of his plays. Ah well, now what was I talking about?'

'The murderer, will he stop, then, when he gets what he wants?' asked Tavistock.

'I doubt it; he may not even know what he wants, and if it's power, the old sort that is, however much he has will never be enough. That's the reason why the English Druids failed so badly: they went too far and started killing their own. A bloodbath rather than a ritual.'

Mannanan stood up and stretched. Birds still sang amongst the leaves and the sun still shone warmly on the surrounding graves but Bob and Tavistock both suddenly felt cold. They both turned towards the old man, only to find a faint mist, like dust motes spiralling towards the sun.

Bob sat in his office and pored through the missing person files he had bullied the long suffering Brian Clague into obtaining. He had also gathered all the post mortem information available and had sent Caroline, the new WPC, round to the library to see if there were any books on early paganism.

Caroline and Brian entered the small room almost simultaneously, both bowed under with files and books of varying sizes and degrees of cleanliness.

'Just put them down and then go and get a cuppa. We all have a lot of work to get through, oh and mine's tea, milk, two sugars.'

Later, sipping his tea thoughtfully, Bob was painfully aware that his two aides were treating him with the careful patience of the average mental care assistant. Although he had to admit that if they only knew even half of the truth, they would be screaming for the Doc to sign him up for a couple of months rest and relaxation in Ballamona, the local mental health establishment.

'I suppose you both want to know why we are ferreting around in the occult and not pulling every known weirdo in?' He looked from one blank face to the other and sighed. This was going to take some time but if he couldn't convince these two then he hadn't got a cat in hell's chance of convincing the Boss.

'So, what do we have so far? Brian?'

'Two bodies, Sir; both have had their throats cut with a sharp curved knife, or at least forensic say that the second body was definitely cut with a curved knife and the first body could have been. Apparently the decomposition of the first body makes it more difficult to tell.'

'How long do they think she's been dead?' asked Caroline, looking up from the papers she had been sorting through.

'Approximately three weeks, according to the tissue report and the age and state of the insect and parasitic life found, living in, on or within the deceased,' Brian replied.

'Right then, team, let's just assume for the sake of argument that both crimes are connected in some way. Caroline, did you find anything out about ritual killings which you think may have any bearing on body number two?' Bob asked, twiddling a pencil around in his tea to loosen the sugar which had solidified at the bottom of his cooling mug.

'Well, the British Druids, Sir, they used to hang their sacrificial victims up by their ankles and then cut their throats. The blood was then collected in a cauldron. It was their belief that the blood then had certain magical properties.' She looked over at Brian who was staring at her as if she had grown two heads. 'Especially if smeared over your own body. At other times the blood was allowed to go straight into the ground to appease the Gods of the Earth, in particular Baal. There were other things as well. For instance, sometimes they used to remove the scalp and hang it from their helmets to give them power over their enemies, especially if it was an enemy scalp.'

'You have got to be joking! You'll be telling me next they stuck the heads in the cauldron and made soup!' Brian shuddered and Caroline nodded ghoulishly.

'They did, in Ireland!' she said with a certain degree of relish.

'OK, you two, that's enough. Brian, calm down, and Caroline, go and get some more tea.'

Brian began to read through the missing persons list, crossing off the names of those no longer missing. By the time Caroline returned bearing yet more tea and a small box of Kit Kats, he had whittled the list down to two. Bob reached for the list with one hand and his mug of tea with the other; two spoons stood to attention in the mug.

'Very funny! Which one of you wants a new career in alternative comedy then?'

Caroline and Brian sat in smug silence. Bob glared at them both and then waving the list in front of them settled back in his chair. Springs groaned metallically and for a brief moment the room was devoid of all noise.

Brian and Caroline exchanged conspiratorial glances and waited for him to give them the benefit of his experience.

'Now then, children, sit back and let your old Uncle Bob explain things as I now see them. We have an elderly lady who allows herself to be tied to something, the lab reckon posts of some sort, in order to have her throat cut. We then have a young lad of about nineteen or twenty, physically fit and healthy, who takes all his clothes off, climbs up a tree, allows someone to tie him by the ankles to said tree and then allows said someone to cut his throat. According to this report neither victim showed any sign of struggling against their bonds or made any attempt to defend themselves. Neither victim was sexually abused, both were found naked and no clothing was recovered at either of the crime scenes. By the way it looks like the boy might be Arthur MacKenzie, commis chef at one of the local hotels. His father is flying over from Aberdeen to identify him as we speak. The old lady could be Brenda

MIST

Skilliton from Ballashedal Farm, Maughold. The neighbours reported her missing about three weeks ago, so the time fits but we won't know for certain until her son returns from America tomorrow. I've already had a lengthy chat with him on the phone and he's given his permission for us to snoop around as much as we like. To be perfectly honest, from the photographs we found when the initial search team went through Mrs Skilliton's cottage, it does look very much as if she's our number one corpse.'

'And neither victim had any connection to the other?' Brian asked.

'Not as far as we can tell.'

'Do you think they could have been drugged, Sir? In one of the books it gives a list of herbs and fungi they used to use to quieten the victim, although they said some of them were hypnotised as well.'

'A combination of natural drugs and hypnosis. Caroline, I believe you may have something there. Right, you two go round and talk to anyone who knew either of them. See if we can find someone who knew them both. Go and look through everything they had like letters, diaries, notebooks, anything with names and addresses. The other thing is, if the old biddy is Miss Skilliton, forensic are pretty certain that she wasn't killed at home, no sign of human blood anywhere. About, three hundred mangy cats but no blood, or at least no human blood. So we need to find the other scene of crime. As soon as we have confirmation of identity the Boss is going public. I can't believe that on an island of over seventy thousand terminal skeeters nobody saw or heard anything.'

Caroline and Brian began clearing their notes and files. Bob moved to the window and rested his cheek against the glass. Logic told him that somebody somewhere would come forward; it was just that intuition told him otherwise.

Later that same day, Caroline and Brian were given the task of going through the late Arthur Mackenzie's small bedsit before his father would be allowed to collect his son's personal effects. They paused on the threshold, both curiously reluctant to move. Brian shrugged his shoulders. If he wanted promotion, this was something he would have to get used to, so he willed his body into action and started searching for the books and letters his superior had asked for. Caroline wandered across the torn and faded carpet and began to inspect the small collection of books piled in haphazard towers next to the single bed. The bed had been shoved in the corner, clothes hung on hangers which in turn hung on a length of clothes line stretched between the window frame and the wooden cornice above the bed.

Carefully they inspected cupboards and shelves, making notes and searching desperately for something, anything, that could help them find a young man's killer. Both had become painfully aware that Arthur had only been a few years younger than themselves and that they could have met him and passed him by in any of the clubs and pubs that most of the youth in Douglas frequented.

Caroline found herself holding tapes and CDs she had in her own flat, Arthur's taste in music being much the same as hers. He even had the same cookery books on the shelves and the paperbacks stacked in piles were almost identical to her own. It was when she found a pile of old postcards relating to a trip to Edinburgh earlier in the year that she realised with a start that here was someone who had gone to see the same shows and exhibitions as she had. Here was someone she could have known and liked.

The doorbell rang, disturbing the quiet concentration of the room. Caroline looked at Brian who shrugged.

'I didn't think the father was due yet?'

'He isn't. Bob said we should ring and let him know when we've finished here. It's not Bob either, because he's gone off to see that writer friend of his.'

The doorbell rang again. Brian rose to his feet and together they cautiously opened the door. Standing on the other side clutching a collection of books and magazines stood a man. He looked to be in his mid thirties and he also looked extremely surprised.

'Is Arthur in?' he asked. 'I'm from the flat upstairs. I've come to return these.' He looked from one to the other. 'Is anything wrong?' he asked.

MIST

Brian cleared his throat and began searching pockets for his warrant card. Caroline watching him, produced her own plastic identification wallet from her shoulder bag and flicked it open. The stranger blinked and swallowed nervously.

'You're police officers,' the man stated, looking from one to the other. They stared back at him.

'I'm afraid Arthur won't be needing those.' Brian pointed to the books and looked to Caroline for help.

Caroline blinked, trying not to show the surprise that she knew both she and Brian felt. The murder of young Arthur had shocked the Island to its core and here was someone who appeared to have missed all the excitement completely. After a short thoughtful pause she spoke. 'Arthur died a while back and we've just been sorting things out for his father.'

'Oh, I see. I didn't know; I've been on a course for the bank I work for, in London. Yes, well, I can see that you're busy so I'll leave you to it.' The man blinked quickly and turned almost blindly towards the stairwell. A book fell from his hands followed by the collection of magazines. Quickly Caroline moved to pick up the falling items. Straightening up she almost bumped heads with him as he bent to try to pick up the same book. Their hands touched and as she looked into his eyes which were a clear piercing blue, the irises very black, she felt herself attracted to him. There was something intense and even oddly dangerous in the atmosphere between them, a magnetism which she had never felt with anyone else before. Brian made a slight movement to close the door of Arthur's room and the moment was lost. The man, suddenly awkward, stammered his thanks and smiled at her. Brian felt a frisson of something run down his back; it felt uncomfortably like jealousy.

'Look, you've had a bit of shock.' Caroline looked at the man enquiringly.

'Paul,' he said, answering the question in her eyes. 'My name is Paul, Paul Stone.' He held out his hand and she shook it, her hand trembling slightly.

'Caroline, Caroline Howard. Look, would you mind if we go up to your flat and ask you a few questions about Arthur? Frankly, anything you can remember at this stage, anything at all might help us with our investigation.'

Paul stood in the doorway and looked from one to the other, his eyes watchful and uncertain. Making a visible effort, he nodded his agreement. Brian locked the door of Arthur's room and followed them both up the stairs. In Paul's flat, which seemed to cover the entire top floor, Paul made them all some tea and then motioned for them to take a seat. Paul himself sat on the edge of a leather covered, modern, grey sofa. Caroline sat opposite in a matching armchair and looked uneasily around. The leather suite was one which Brian had seen in a store in Douglas months before and had hated on sight. He'd wondered at the time just what sort of idiot would buy something that 'naff' and now he knew.

'You said Arthur died. Just how did he die? It wasn't that wretched bike of his, was it? He was always tinkering with it, and he drove too fast.'

'No, it wasn't an accident; Arthur was murdered,' Brian said, his voice flat and his eyes watchful for any sign of reaction to his words. Paul, clearly startled, blinked rapidly and with slightly shaky hands attempted to pour tea from a stainless steel teapot into mugs. Trying desperately to appear normal, Paul looked up and asked, 'Milk?' Brian nodded and Paul bent back towards the tea tray in front of him. 'Sugar?'

'Yes, one, please.'

Carefully Brian sipped his tea, notebook at the ready.

Paul handed a mug to Caroline and sat back. Thoughtfully he stroked a chin covered in a faint shadow of stubble, probably designer stubble, thought Brian a trifle meanly.

'I don't really know what to say, we've been friends for the last year, ever since he came over here. We go out together most weekends, theatre, cinema, the odd meal. I can give you a list of mutual friends if you like. Apart from that we go out, I mean we went out, for lunch most Sundays if Arthur wasn't on duty. He didn't do drugs, didn't drink any more than anyone else. Most people liked him, he was funny, you know, could tell really good jokes and he did this really amazing impersonation of Billy Connolly in an Indian restaurant.' He laughed, remembering, but catching sight of Brian's poker face he stopped and looked down at the carpet. Tears welled up and he blew his nose loudly.

'Arthur wouldn't hurt a fly; there really must be some kind of mistake.'

There was silence as each tried to search for words and failed.

'Look here's my card. If you think of anything, just give me a ring, eh.' Caroline handed over the small card and Brian rose from the black canvas director's chair he had been perching on.

As they reached the door, Paul turned to them and said rather hesitantly, 'There was one thing; Arthur said he had a new friend. They met up at the college, he did this course on Thursday nights. Anyway he said he'd met this guy up there. I never met him. Don't even know his name and I don't want to.'

'Why?' Brian asked, making a note to check the college lists for Thursdays.

'He wanted Arthur to hold some sort of séance. Arthur came round about a month ago with this board and some books on the occult. I told him it was a load of rubbish and we had our one and only really big row. We made up again about a week later but he wouldn't talk about it at all after that. Sorry, I can't tell you any more. He did tell me they were going camping to make a video, sort of Blair witch project, only Manx. I went on this course shortly afterwards but if there was a video it should have them both on it.'

Brian and Caroline looked at each other and sighed. Perhaps Uncle Bob did have something after all; at any rate they would have to search Arthur's belongings again. They both thanked Paul, Caroline's thanks being patently more genuine than Brian's. Quickly they retraced their steps and again entered the small bedsit. Cupboards were searched and drawers were carefully turned upside down. After about ten minutes Brian, who had dragged a chair over to the minuscule kitchen area and was searching the top of the one and only wall cupboard, discovered the ouija board, wrapped in a check tablecloth and covered in what looked like very old blood.

Caroline quaked inwardly as he handed it over to her. She was beginning to have very serious doubts about the wisdom of a career in the police, if this was going to happen on a regular basis. So far her short stint on the Force had centred around petty crime, the taking of copious notes, and the visiting of most of the Island's schools, not grubbing around in other people's dirty laundry and dabbling with the occult.

26th April

Bob sat in the passenger seat of Tavistock's car and watched huge green waves pounding the sea wall. Rocks and pebbles were strewn across the road together with a jumble of seaweed and what looked like half a tree.

The driver's door opened and Tavistock climbed breathlessly in, holding onto the door with grim determination as the wind whipped round and tried to tear it from her grasp.

'Bit fresh out there, isn't it?' Bob observed as he watched a gull struggling to land against the elements.

'Do you do courses in the Force for stating the obvious?' asked Tavistock, adjusting her seat belt.

'Nope, only in avoiding going out in anything more than a force four and that,' Bob pointed to the waves crashing over the sea wall,'is at least a seven! Besides, it wasn't me that got the wrong house, was it?'

Bob folded his arms and continued to watch the marine drama going on outside. Tavistock felt a sudden longing to thump him but instead she counted silently to ten, undid her seat belt, muttered, 'Right you sod,' and said, 'The lady we are about to meet lives in the thatched cottage on the right, so we can leave the car here and walk. There's nowhere to park outside and it's only a narrow road. By the way, that course you went on, long time ago was it?' She smiled sweetly and with a feeling of having won a minor skirmish opened the car door and waited for Bob to get out.

They staggered like a couple of drunks across the road, narrowly missing a fast-moving red Nissan Micra which neither had heard and Bob only just saw out of the corner of his eye in time.

'Road hog,' he shouted at the retreating tail lights.

'Get lost did you?' shrieked a white haired old woman in a bright purple anorak and the largest pair of yellow wellingtons Bob had ever seen. The woman pushed aside a black iron gate set in a green hedge of hebe and fuchsia and gestured for them to follow her.

Once inside the low thatched cottage and seated before a bright log fire, Bob began slowly to dry out and to take stock of his surroundings. Tavistock had rung earlier that day to say that she had managed to find the address of a local woman who was reputed to be one of the few 'Wise Women' still left on the Island. Her name was Morag and she was the secretary of the Pagan Society. Looking around he spotted several interesting looking bottles and on the shelves which ran along one entire wall, some very strange looking implements and books.

Moving his eye along one of the shelves, reading the yellowing labels on some of the jars, he came across the title 'Eye of Newt'. Next to it sat a small black cauldron and a bag made of coarse sacking with the words 'Frogs Toes' written in capitals on the front in black ink.

'Bugger me!' he said, looking around quickly for Tavistock, who had previously disappeared through a side door with the lady he presumed was called Morag.

'If I'd known you were that way inclined, I'd have asked my son Peter to join us,' said Morag, removing the 'Frogs Toes' from his hands and gently placing them back on the shelf. Bob felt his face begin to glow a light beetroot and began stammering apologies. He felt as he had when seven years old and caught red handed by his great-aunt in the process of tucking into a plate of illicit jam tarts.

Morag shooed him over to the fire and thrust a large mug of tea into his hands. Tavistock was already sitting on a large oak settle sipping her tea and grinning in a way he imagined the average Cheshire Cat would.

'Now, young man, before you walk off with any funny ideas, those things you found on the shelf are props for my granddaughter's school play, *Macbeth*. I'm not a witch, I'm a herbalist and produce homeopathic remedies for all sorts of things. Hence the large selection of dried herbs and other raw materials. That small machine next to you is a pill press, not an instrument of carnal

MIST

pleasure, so put it down and stop fiddling with things that aren't anything to do with you. Tavistock tells me you have some questions to ask me in relation to the recent murders, so why don't you start asking and if I can help in any way, I will.'

Bob sipped his tea cautiously; it tasted fine, just like tea should. For one horrible minute he'd wondered if it was raspberry or rosehip or something really weird.

'We think the murders were of a ritual nature, possibly pagan in origin. I've brought a few photographs of the second body in situ, so to speak. Could you have a look and see if you can spot anything which may tie in with, well, anything?'

Morag looked at the photographs, gradually pursing her lips together until Bob thought they would disappear completely.

'Well, I really thought the papers were sensationalising things again; they weren't were they?' Bob shook his head and waited. Morag sighed and bent her head back to the photographs. She winced visibly, a shudder of distaste running through her body.

'It looks like an early Druid sacrifice to the local God or Goddess of the Earth; you see the blood is draining directly into the earth. Did they struggle at all?'

'No, we wondered if they had been drugged?'

'That's possible, yes. The Druids, or priests if you want to call them that, used to prepare the victims for sacrificing to their Gods in a combination of ways, mainly fasting, drugs and hypnosis. You see, they wouldn't see it as murder; it was a ritual, like sacrificing a chicken or the cutting of a bull's throat as the Romans used to do, during their adoration of Mithras. You see the way the ropes are knotted; that's so that the victim could be lowered nearer the ground so that he wouldn't swing and spill blood into the trees. Afterwards the body would be hauled back and allowed to swing free. Whoever did this would be naked as well, except for talismans and other jewellery. I gather that there was nothing else hanging except for the boy's body?'

'No, nothing, no clothes, no weapon, nothing.'

'I presume that there was no sexual interference of any kind?'

'Nothing,' Bob stated flatly, carefully keeping his voice as neutral as possible. 'Whoever did this just cut his throat and for what? With a crime of passion, even violence, you can try to understand why it was done but this! It's a waste, a waste of a life, of our time, of his.'

'I'm not so sure.' Morag stared past Bob and suddenly moved with alacrity to the bookshelf on one side of the fireplace and after searching for a few minutes she returned bearing a large dusty volume. Carefully wiping the dust off with her sleeve, she sat down next to Bob and began to turn the mud-coloured pages. Coming upon an illustration of a hill and an old man holding a staff, she placed the book on Bob's lap and tapped the picture gleefully.

'That is Mannanan Mac Lir, our very own local deity. It was believed by some that he sleeps below the earth and that he can only awaken if the Islanders return to the old religion.'

'Interesting,' Bob muttered, trying not to catch Tavistock's eye.

'Actually, it isn't quite as daft as it sounds. Mannanan disappeared from most stories and legends at about the same time as the early Irish Christians arrived on the Island. The legend is based on the belief that Mannanan was bewitched by one of their followers. This lady lured him to a cave within a lonely hill, relieved him of his powers and sent him to sleep. Of course the story was written at about the time that the story of the *Morte d'Arthur* became popular.'

'Could you say that last bit again in English?' asked Bob who was trying to work out where the hill was because even with the usual artistic licence, he thought he recognised it.

'The legend of King Arthur. You know the bit where the wizard Merlin is seduced and is incarcerated in a cave by his lover.'

'Now that's what I call plagiarism,' laughed Tavistock.

'Doesn't look a bit like me!' said Mannanan who had quietly materialised beside Morag. 'And I never did that!' he muttered crossly whilst reading over her shoulder. 'Well, I might have done that but only if they annoyed me!'

Bob, who was finding it difficult to keep a straight face, looked appealingly at Tavistock, who was trying to cover her own laughter by coughing loudly into a tartan handkerchief.

'Are you all right, my love?' Morag asked gently. 'You just rest

MIST

there and I'll make us another nice cup of tea.' Morag quickly gathered up their mugs and moved off into the gloom. A door shut and they could hear the sounds of a kettle being filled and of tins being opened.

'What the bloody hell are you doing here?' Bob hissed, wiping the tears from his face.

'I got bored. Besides it's a long time since I've had any truck with the likes of her. Her great grandmother's grandmother was as batty as a fruitcake. Made a positive fortune in selling love potions and charms to the young and desperate, the not so young but very desperate and the frankly past it!'

'Oh!'

'Obviously runs in the family.'

'Look, if she's a witch, why can't she see you?'

'Because she's not a witch. She's a pagan and a herbalist and before you ask I wouldn't have slept with her dotty ancestor if you'd put a bag over her head and paid me! Now she really looked like a witch, louse invested hair, hairy warts and black teeth. Your great, great, great etc, grandmother on the other hand was long limbed, auburn haired, green eyed and had a chest you could sleep in.'

'Be quiet, you two, she's coming back.'

They all turned and listened to the sounds of teaspoons and crockery rattling on a tray. Suddenly the doorbell rang, a dog barked loudly and they heard Morag open the back door and say, 'Oh, it's you. Look, come back later; I've got visitors, the Police, about that murder. We can have a word then.' Sounds reached them of the visitor saying something about milk churns and then the door closed and Morag returned with the tray of tea things.

'Nice young man that, but a bit simple if you know what I mean. Now where were we?'

'The legend of Mannanan Mac Lir,' said Tavistock.

'Ah yes, well, you see I think that maybe your murderer just wants to wake him up, and by this ritual of pouring blood onto the earth he hopes that the earth will release its prisoner.'

'What I really think is that some nutter has been reading too many Bernard Cornwells!' Bob grimaced and picked up his tea.

'Perhaps, the thing is, from the look of these pictures I'd say he actually believes he can do it and of course until he succeeds he'll continue.'

'Oh great! And do you have any idea as to when and where?' asked Bob.

'Possibly 1st May, May Day, and as he's already used Druidale, one of the other ancient sites. I'll write you out a list if you like. You see, he doesn't see this as murder but as something akin to going down to a church and lighting a candle. The other thing is, I would make a rough guess that he has killed before, several times, that he was obsessed with the occult at an early age and that his first killing was done when he was quite young, possibly before reaching his teens.' Morag took a sip of tea and continued, 'It may even have been a member of his own family; the really powerful and most influential druids were very keen to have no mortal ties that could be used against them.'

'Sorry?' Bob sat slightly stunned, eyebrows almost crossed over the bridge of his nose.

'For instance, if you spilt the blood of a child you had power over the parents, and vice versa. You'll find that most records containing any reference to the late Celtic priests had them arriving on the scene of conflict, say at a battle, with followers but no family.'

Bob whistled softly; this would indeed tie in with the police profiler's assumption that their madman was outwardly sane, on a specific mission and had no ties or immediate family.

'Right, well, this has all been very useful and I shall of course include all the relevant details in my report. Come along, Tavistock, and thanks for the tea.'

Bob and Tavistock left, carefully avoiding each other's eyes and in particular Mannanan's who was scowling furiously and swearing in some ancient tongue under his breath. They made it to the car, shut the doors and the pent up almost hysterical laughter they had both been desperately trying to control erupted. Mannanan sat in the back and glared at them.

'I suppose one of you would like to share this with me?' he asked almost petulantly. 'I don't suppose either of you have considered

MIST

that the old bat may be right and that some daft sod is just trying to say hello! I've guarded this Isle for over two thousand years against this sort of madness and now it's here, all you two can do is laugh!'

'Look, it's not you, it's the irony of the situation, that's all.' Bob breathed deeply and looked towards the gloomy cliffs.

'Bloody Nora, the first of May; that's not very far away. The only thing we know about this case is that someone somewhere is being marked down and maybe has only a matter of days to live. And there is absolutely nothing I can do because I haven't the foggiest idea of where to bloody well start!'

30th April

Caroline and Brian moved cautiously around the small Manx cottage that had been home to Brenda Skilliton for nearly eighty years. The motley collection of cats belonging to the late owner had already been removed by someone from the MSPCA but their unmistakable odour lingered. Innumerable trays of cat litter were strewn around the room, under chairs and tables. Small dishes and saucers of dried cat food and mouldering fish also littered surfaces already covered in an array of crocheted doilies and china ornaments. Carefully Brian moved to the window and after a few minutes of tugging and pushing managed to open the grime-encrusted glass a few inches. Waves of cold sea air blew about the room scattering dust and moving the stale air towards the chimney breast. Caroline breathed a sigh of relief. She hated cats and the smell had made her feel increasingly sick. Silently she opened the kitchen door and gagged at the stench of rotting food, in particular a bag of opened coley fillets which had oozed across the old wooden draining board. Hurriedly she fled to the back door and after turning the heavy key and pushing the iron bolt across she finally managed to escape and sink onto an old bench outside.

Brian found her a few minutes later huddled against the cold and desperately chewing extra strong mints. Silently he offered her a cigarette, which she declined with a smile and a nod. They sat in silence while the air in the cottage cleared, Caroline chewing and Brian breathing in the acrid smoke of his cigarette.

'How can people live like that?' she asked, gesturing behind her.

'Dunno, maybe it just happens over the years. My Gran got like that in the end. She used to just wander off on her own. All hours of the day and night, she liked a bit of a walk did Gran.'

'What happened to her?'

MIST

'The doctor got a bit worried and Dad got fed up collecting her from the police station so they put her in one of them residential homes, the theory being that there they could keep a better eye on her. They were very good really, did trips out and bingo, food was all right too from what I saw. Thing is, Gran never really liked people and couldn't abide being helped either. She died about four months later. Mum reckoned she just lost interest in things and turned her face to the wall. She had this big old fleabag of a cat called Bagpuss, actually looked just like that one on the kiddies' programme, know the one I mean?' Caroline nodded. 'Gran loved that cat; he was her only friend after Grandpa died. He used to wait for her at the bus stop when she'd gone to the shops, slept on her bed every night. They didn't allow pets in the home so we used to smuggle him in in an old picnic basket; it was the only time I remember Gran smiling. Funny things you remember, I must have been only about nine or ten at the time. Living alone is sometimes from choice, you know, and it's not as if old Brenda didn't have a good innings, I mean, look at all them photos everywhere!'

'Do you think it's cleared yet?'

'Wouldn't have thought so, give it another ten minutes or so.'

Bob, rounding the corner of the cottage fifteen minutes later, found his two assistants drinking coffee and quietly chatting. Slowly he crept up behind them.

'Morning, Sir, want a coffee? There's about a cup left, my mum always makes loads.'

'Brian, how the ... '

'Did I know you were there, Sir?'

'Yes.'

'Saw your reflection in them glass cloches, Sir.'

'So tell me, my little Munchkins,' Bob asked, as he eased himself onto the bench and reached out for the polystyrene cup of coffee Brian had offered him. 'You just tell your old Uncle Bob why you are sitting here in an aura of tranquillity, whilst any clues we may have are still sitting in there!' He pointed to the open back door and looked enquiringly at them both.

'We were just waiting for the air to clear, Sir. We think the old lady was killed, or taken away, before she'd finished feeding the cats.'

'Ah, I see your problem, opened tins of festering rabbit, eh?'

'Worse, fish! coley fillets!'

'Better make it another half hour then,' Bob said, looking around. 'I suppose we could make a start on that shed over there.'

'Right you are then. Sir, I saw some keys hanging by the door, I'll just go and get them and see if any fit.'

Brian returned, red in the face from holding his breath, with a bunch of assorted keys.

'I think it may take more than half an hour, Sir. The old lady also had a dog.'

Bob and Caroline watched as Brian rubbed something from his eyes.

'A dog?'

'Yes, Sir, small terrier, I think; difficult to tell, as its head's missing.'

'What!'

'I dropped the keys, and when I bent down to pick them up, I saw it under the kitchen table.'

'But surely Forensic would have found it?' Caroline said.

'Not if someone came back and put it there.' Bob thoughtfully stroked his chin. 'Well, it looks like our friendly psycho came back to drop off the pooch. I wonder if he came back for anything else and more importantly, if he left anything behind. Caroline, call the Office and get Forensic back, and while you're doing that, Brian and I are going to go and have a word with the neighbours again.'

'Another scone, Inspector? Or would you prefer some of this caramel slice?'

'No, no, thank you Mrs Collister, I couldn't eat another thing.'

'Call me Mona, Inspector. How about you, Constable, try one of these iced fancies.'

Brian who had already eaten two scones, a cherry tartlet and a large golden flapjack passed his plate over at a silent nod from his

MIST

superior. His stomach quaked inwardly and he began to nibble the proffered cake very, very slowly.

'Would you like any more tea, Inspector?' asked Ted Collister. Ted stood in the archway between the small sitting room and their even smaller kitchen. It wasn't often that the Collisters had visitors and both Ted and Mona had no intention of letting either of them go before they had observed all the social niceties.

'No, no, thank you. The reason we have both come round to see you is to ask you both a few more questions concerning your neighbour Brenda Skilliton. That is if you don't mind and could spare us a bit of your valuable time.'

'Not at all, Inspector, not at all, only too pleased to help.' Ted moved to the one remaining empty chair and sank into its depths. Bob watched in fascination. He had never seen household objects eating people before but the Collister's deep red upholstered suite appeared to be doing just that. Eagerly Ted and Mona Collister waited for him to start, their hands clasped gently in their respective laps and their heads held to one side, for all the world like a pair of aged budgerigars. Brian, with a certain amount of relief, put his plate down on the glass-topped coffee table and fumbled in his pocket for a notepad and pen.

'Is there anything you could tell us about Brenda that you haven't told us already, anything at all? Has anyone been seen walking round her property since her death, say over the last couple of days?'

A short silence ensued as Ted and Mona thought. The grandfather clock in the hall chimed the hour; springs whirred and the clunking sounds of brass weights falling carried around the house. The gas fire popped and the large brown tabby cat spread-eagled over the hearthrug stretched and rolled over so that his white stomach could toast gently. Outside the wind whistled past net clad windows; a vehicle with a diesel engine drove by. It stopped further down the lane; doors opened and closed with metallic bangs and voices were heard shouting unintelligible instructions.

'Ah good, Forensic are finally here,' thought Bob.

'Well, I don't think anyone has come round recently, except for that reporter chap and the man from the radio. You remember, dear, the young one with the short hair and the fruity voice, the one our Alice listens to.'

Ted scratched his chin and after a few minutes of careful thought said, 'There was that young man from the estate agents. Now let me think, it was about three or maybe four days ago.'

'Estate agents?' Bob and Brian looked at each other, both knowing that no one had as yet been instructed to do anything concerning the property, most especially since they had specifically asked the advocate involved with Brenda's estate to leave everything as it was for the time being: at least until they had exhausted all possibility of finding any further clues as to her untimely and horrific death.

'Oh yes, he came round while you were out at the WI, dear, and asked to borrow the keys. Now let me think, he had some letter, signed by the advocate, to say it was all right and one of those cards to say who he was. I did check, you see; I mean you can't just let anyone in, can you.' Ted looked anxiously at the two policemen.

'You have a spare set of keys? Would you mind telling me how you got them?' Bob smiled broadly; he didn't want to scare this little thin man but he had the feeling that if he didn't probe a little further a few more clues would vanish into the ether.

'Brenda gave them to me with the letter,' Mona said, patting her husband's hand. 'She wanted me to have a spare set in case she locked herself out.'

'I thought she kept a spare under the watering can,' Ted stated, looking slightly bemused. 'I thought we had her keys so you could feed the cats and look after things when she went to stay with her son in Bournemouth?'

'When was this?' Brian asked.

'Boxing Day; she stayed with him for some family reunion over the New Year. I just thought she forgot to ask for them back and then when she died we just held onto them. Well, no one asked for their return, did they?' Ted nervously pulled an ear lobe and looked to his wife again for reassurance.

'It's all right, dear. You see, Inspector, Brenda told me she'd seen

MIST

someone she used to know. She said he'd done something very wrong as a child. She didn't want anyone to know because she said everyone deserved a second chance.' Bob held his breath and Brian looked up. 'She never said what it was, mind. I suppose, knowing Brenda, it could have been anything from stealing sweets to being rude to the Vicar.'

Bob felt like a suddenly deflated balloon. Brian sighed and bent again to his notebook.

'It's all in the letter; she told me to give it to Christopher, that's her son in Bournemouth, if anything should happen to her. That's why she gave me the keys. She didn't want him to get into the house while she was out; the cats or something. She really worried about it, only she would never say why. To be honest, she was very odd over the last couple of months, kept seeing things in the bushes. I know I put it somewhere in the dresser here. Silly me, you know I'd clean forgotten about it until now. I don't suppose Christopher would mind if you had a look at it first.' Mona began to pull out various drawers, dislodging a quantity of old bills, photographs, bits of ribbon and a variety of coloured plastic bands. Finally she turned, holding a long brown envelope which she handed to Bob with a small apologetic smile.

Bob who had while she'd been talking put on a pair of clear plastic gloves, nodded to Brian to do the same. Mona watched them, a faint frown on her face. 'Do you want me to wear something too, only I've got some new Marigolds in the kitchen?'

Bob shook his head and then with great care opened the envelope and removed the sheets of white closely written paper. He began to read and as he read he passed them over to Brian. Finally when he'd come to the end he closed his eyes and said a silent prayer of thanks.

After several minutes he opened them and eyed both of the Collisters with a certain degree of caution.

'This estate agent, could you give me a description? What was he wearing, make of car, voice, anything.'

'Well.' Ted looked to his wife, trepidation written over his grey features. 'He was just a young man, he had a suit and tie and a black briefcase, nicely spoken. I think he had a Manchester accent? Brown hair, glasses; oh yes, and he drove a little red car.'

Bob sighed and Brian carefully folded the letter up and handed it back.

'Thank you both very much for your help and for the letter which I'd like to hang on to if I may. If there is anything else you remember, anything at all, just give me a ring.' He handed over a card with his number on it and stood up. 'Please don't worry, Mr Collister, you didn't do anything wrong but if anyone else comes round could you let us know immediately and I think you had better return the keys to the lawyers dealing with the estate. Brian can give you the details, or he could hand them over himself, save you the trouble.'

Ted and Mona looked at each other, Mona nodded and Ted disappeared into the kitchen. He returned with a large bunch of keys, which he handed over to Bob with a certain amount of relief.

Bob and Brian moved to the door and again expressed their gratitude for the tea and cakes.

Standing outside the small modern bungalow, they buttoned up against the brisk April air and marched off towards Brenda's cottage.

'Sir, is it my imagination or are there more keys on that bunch than the ones in the cottage?'

'No, Brian, for once our joint minds think alike. We're going to go through every lock in the place and after what we've both read, I hope to God our little bogus estate agent hasn't managed to get there first.'

Caroline stood at the bedroom window of Brenda's cottage watching soft white clouds scudding across the sky. Behind them loomed a black front of low cumulus. More rain. She turned to the group of men searching the room for fresh prints and asked if she could open the window. They nodded and reaching up to release the catch she noticed a small blue book, taped to the back of the wooden pelmet.

'Geoff, have you got a moment?' Geoff de-morphed from the

MIST

group and walked over. She pointed quietly to her find. 'Was that there last time?'

Geoff scratched his neck and after a few moments admitted that they hadn't actually looked there yet. Carefully they removed the tape and the book, placing both in protective plastic. Caroline could feel excitement seeping through her cold body; she couldn't wait to tell the others.

Noises rose from the kitchen below sounding very much like a herd of marauding rhinos, stripping trees. Footsteps thumped up the bare wooden stairs until finally Bob Callow erupted into the bedroom trailing long strands of cobweb and dead weed. Caroline blinked as a large fat spider moved across the balding head and jumped off, narrowly missing Brian who appeared suddenly behind him.

'Evening, folks, anybody found anything interesting? No? Fine, let's just have these floorboards up then. Brian and I have already decimated the kitchen,' Bob said, rubbing the inside of his left ear with a short grimy fingernail.

'So we heard,' Geoff muttered, trying not to watch the earwig walking across Bob's shoulder.

'Come on, Caroline, stop gawking and get hunting; we need to find a book of some kind, according to this.' Bob waved the letter at her and began to heave a chest of drawers away from the skirting board, dislodging more spiders, woodlice and a large glossy beetle.

Before either Caroline or Geoff could show him the book they had found, Brian began to tear up the floorboards with a large crowbar he kept in his car. And the youngest member of the forensic team discovered a very large, very irate mother rat with a nest of little hairless babies behind the wardrobe he'd just moved. The mother rodent attacked with a hiss, yellow teeth bared, the youth jumped on the bed, the bed collapsed and in the ensuing confusion a loud deep bass voice shouted, 'What the bloody hell is going on?'

There was silence, broken by a low growl emitted by a huge chocolate and cream coloured German shepherd, which almost flew across the room towards the attacking rodent. The rat was seized,

MIST

tossed into the air, caught and despatched in one bite. The baby rats were eaten and the dog, tail thumping, returned to its master.

Bob cleared his throat and rummaged in his pocket for his warrant card. Moving towards the stranger, he flapped open the plastic wallet and keeping careful watch on the dog, who was trying to look innocent with a tail sticking out of his mouth, began to explain.

Brian lifted his pint glass and drained the last warm brown drop. There was to his mind nothing like a good pint of best bitter and this, he had to admit, was nothing like it. The only thing in its favour was that the angry stranger, who had turned out to be Brenda Skilliton's son, was paying for it. Caroline sipped her ginger beer carefully; aware that it was her turn on taxi duty, she would have given almost anything for a glass of cold white wine. Perhaps, she thought, when Paul comes round we can share the one in the fridge. Brian, watching her, saw the faint smile playing on her lips and felt a stab of something which felt almost like jealousy.

The first time Paul Stone had telephoned the office to arrange a meeting with Caroline, Brian had assumed they were meeting to discuss something Paul had remembered about Arthur; he'd even offered to go with her. A week later flowers had appeared on her desk and when he'd made some comment about bankers she'd flown at him. It was only the timely intervention of 'Uncle Bob' that had cooled the atmosphere down. Brian had since kept his views to himself and it had only been outside Brenda's cottage that morning that their old easy banter had resumed.

He looked down at his empty glass and remonstrated in his head over the daftness of feeling anything for his colleague. Slowly he looked up, meeting Bob's eyes.

'Same again?' he asked, avoiding his superior's shrewd appraisal.

There was a low throated growl from under the table. Bob coughed loudly and Christopher Skilliton opened another packet of cheese and onion flavoured crisps and passed them under the table to the ever hungry canine whom they had discovered was called Lucifer. Carefully Brian left their table, anxious not to draw

MIST

attention to the fact that there was a dog under it. They were all well aware of the landlord's firmly held views on animals. Bob looked uneasily around. 'So far so good,' he thought.

'Tell me again, Chris, just exactly why can't the hound of the Baskervilles stay in the car?'

'Because he eats the seat covers and chews the steering wheel!'

'Fair comment.'

'Besides it's only a hire car and they weren't exactly overkeen on hiring it out to start with. He went for the manager, you see.'

'Oh, I do indeed see; does he actually bite or is it all bark?' Bob asked, carefully moving his feet away from the crisp-eating hound.

'Mostly bark; he's a big softy really. The kids love him. Mind you, if he thought you were going to attack he'd retaliate.'

Brian returned with a tray of drinks and some more crisps, which he carefully distributed.

'Right then, let's get down to business. Your mother left a note in which she mentioned a lad she'd once known by the name of Juan Moss. Did she say anything at all about recognising him with a friend at some local show or fair? For instance, when she stayed with you and your family at Christmas or did she mention anything over the phone? Quite frankly, anything at all may help.'

Christopher thought carefully. 'No, I can't think of anything. I'm sorry, I can't remember him myself either. I was adopted, you see. Mother took me in when I was about eight or nine. Originally she was my foster mother but we, well, we hit it off and she eventually adopted me. She was strict but she was always there for me, always went to every meeting at school, came to see me in all the plays I was in. There wasn't much in the way of things; she had her husband's pensions and benefits. He must have died a couple of years before I went to live with her. From what she said he worked on the local farms but no one ever spoke about him. I gathered from the lads at school that he drank. He can't have been a pleasant companion. Actually there was something, I think she had a photograph of Juan Moss, his younger brother, and another local lad they used to play with. She kept them in an old biscuit box in the kitchen.'

MIST

'Are you sure?'

'Positive. I rang, a few days before she disappeared, to find out if she'd received the photographs I'd sent her of the kids. She said she had and that she'd put them with the others in the biscuit tin. It had "Melting Moments" written on the front; it was a bit of a family joke.'

'Brian, has anybody found a tin of photos?'

'No, not as yet.'

'You know, it's ironic, isn't it? I finally persuaded the old lady to move to sheltered housing and this happens. I keep thinking that perhaps if I'd insisted she wouldn't have been alone and she might still be alive.' He coughed and blew loudly into a large paper handkerchief.

'Now then, now then. Frankly, I don't reckon it would have made a hap'orth of difference. This chap, whoever he is, would have just hung around and waited for an opportunity. This new accommodation: where was it exactly?'

'It was one of those flats at Saddlemews and before you ask, I was paying for it. Mind you, it's the first time she'd allowed me to pay for anything, except for her fares across to see us all once a year.'

'I don't suppose she mentioned what this lad was supposed to have done?'

'No, not really. She did say that the family hushed it all up, there was a lot of bad feeling about it and I think they moved off the Island. All she did say was that she saw his face and he meant it, what ever "it" was. Sorry; I'm not being much help. I just just find it difficult to believe that anyone would murder someone in their eighties and nearly blind to boot.'

'Hang on, you mean she couldn't see?'

'Yes. She had cataracts in both eyes. The right side was worse than the left, she could hardly see at all out of that one. You must have realised from the state of the place, all that dust and she had that white stick of hers.'

'White stick?'

The old lady woke and tried to focus. Everything was dark, dark and

MIST

fuzzy. She felt tired and drunk. She couldn't remember the last time she had eaten or even how long she had been there. She remembered the voice though. Even now she could hear that soft, cold voice dripping carefully phrased madness into her ears. The room she was in seemed to be full of wood, dank, evil smelling. If evil has a smell, she thought, it would be this mix of fungus, and she sniffed. There was something else, something sweet: the smell of meat left too long, of over ripe pheasant or hare.

Carefully she pulled herself up and stumbling on a sharp object she threw her hands out to save herself and found a smooth long stick. It glowed slightly in the gloom and she felt with her hands for the pile of wood in the furthest corner. Listening for the slightest of sounds she dug into the wood and found the skull. Pausing again to listen she sought out the nail and piece of paper on which she had painstakingly drawn in her own blood, crude letters. If it should be found, perhaps it would stop the man who lurked beyond her prison walls. Perhaps, she thought, it would stop someone from believing in him.

She was aware today that the smell was stronger, so strong in fact that she couldn't concentrate. Slowly she returned the nail and paper to the skull and hid it deep within its wooden grave. She began to move carefully towards the rank odour and at last almost stepped on the plastic bag which contained the smell. For some reason she knew she had to find out what it was. With hands trembling with cold and fear she tore at the plastic. The object rolled into her lap, its shape so familiar that she felt sick and retched helplessly. Her throat was dry; saliva spilled from her mouth in stale dribbles. She felt the soft fur, ignoring the dried blood and decaying flesh. Here was her companion of nearly fifteen years. She rocked gently on her heels and heard a scream that seemed to go on for ever. It was hers and she couldn't stop.

Bob and Tavistock sat around her kitchen table drinking fresh coffee and eating small oddly decorated cakes that the children had made the night before. Mannanan sat quietly on a kitchen unit and looked through the window at the dying light. The trees outside

MIST

shimmered pink and gold, the soft new leaves dancing. It was, he sighed, a beautiful evening. Slowly he turned from the vista of sky and hills and joined the hunched figures at the table.

'Where are the children?' he asked, realising the time and that the house was still in a state of peace.

'George is staying with his friend Alex and Kate and Emily are at their grandparents tonight. Oh, and Richard has some sort of accountants' dinner so he's staying on at the hotel. It's not that he can't drive,' she muttered, giving Bob a sideways glance, 'just that he has difficulty finding the little hole to put the key in.'

'Ah,' said Mannanan, sinking into a pine coloured chair.

'Anyway, tomorrow they all go off on the ferry for a week in Scotland with their cousins and my poor long suffering brother Berlin.'

'Berlin? Tavistock, I hate to ask but just why do you all have such peculiar names?'

'This from a man who thinks Alfreda and Yoric attractive. My parents, who are still completely potty and have been since university, decided in their wisdom to name us after the places in which we were conceived. Which is why my younger brother is called Berlin and my baby sister is called Vienna. When they had me they didn't have that much cash and spent the summer months in a caravan in the West Country.'

'Perhaps it's just as well that the Iron Curtain was still up or you could have been called Petrograd or how about Vladivostock?'

'You are such a funny man, Bob Callow. So now that you have our undivided attention without fear of interruption, could you just get on with whatever it is that you wanted to show both of us?'

'To be honest, something neither of you are actually seeing, because I have never shown you, agreed?' Bob looked from one to the other seeking their acceptance.

Slowly he passed over various sheets of paper, which Tavistock and Mannanan began to read.

'The first copy is that of a letter from the first victim to her son and the second is of the book to which the letter refers.'

MIST

Dear Chris,

I'm not too sure where to begin but if you are reading this, it means that I didn't die of natural causes.

Some time ago, before you came to live with me, I became friends with a young lad. His name was Juan Moss and I believe he murdered his younger brother Liam, who was four at the time. Juan himself was only eight, although I sometimes thought he spoke and acted more like a man of twenty eight. He always said that he was trying to help him out after falling in a rock pool. But I got there first and I could have sworn he was holding the lad under the water. The family moved away and the police had no proof and what could I say?

I wish now I had said something, anything, but at the time I couldn't cause his parents any more pain; they had already lost one son. So how could I cause them to lose the other?

The thing is, Juan is back. I heard him at the village fair. He was buying cakes and he had a young man with him. The lad seemed nice enough; to be honest they sounded happy, oddly enough like lovers.

Yesterday, I leant out of my bedroom window early to listen to the first nestlings in the apple tree, the one you used as Captain Hook's pirate ship. I felt someone watching and looked down. I know no one will believe me, blind as I am, but he was in the garden and he was staring up at me. I felt his presence. All day I refused to go outside and I rang Norma at the shop for my groceries. When the boy delivered them I got him to check the garden. No one was there, but tonight he came back.

Christopher, my dear, I have written it all down in a book, which I will leave in the old place we used to put messages for the fairies. If anything happens to me, see that the police get the book and tell them to open up the old Moss files. Please, my dear boy, take care and give my love to Sally and the children. You will never know what joy you gave me watching you grow up to be someone I could be so proud of.

Your success has made me feel that the early years were worthwhile and I am so glad I lived to see my grandchildren.

May God be with you always.

Your ever loving Mother.

Tavistock looked up from reading the letter, shock written on her features.

'The poor old thing, she sounds terrified. How could someone that young do something like that, he was only eight! That would be like Kate drowning little Emily.' Tavistock shuddered, the nightmarish picture of her children in her mind.

'Evil has no minimum limit, my dear,' Mannanan said. 'I could tell you things about the Druid Apprentices which would make your hair turn white and some of them were only four or five when they took their first rites.'

'The book explains the rest; it seems to have been a kind of diary Brenda Skilliton made at the time and I've copied the relevant pages.'

Tavistock picked up the pages and began to read. Bob wandered over to the window and looked out at the twilight world outside. He felt worried: perhaps it was the content of the book Tavistock was reading or because tomorrow was the first of May and he had a hunch that Juan Moss was still out there, prowling the hills and glens and waiting for the sunrise.

'I wouldn't waste too much sympathy on the lad.' Bob muttered. 'You haven't read the diary and I have. I tell you I never truly believed in the old Victorian belief that a soul could be born bad, but . . . ' He shrugged, letting the words hang in the air between them.

Mannanan sighed and bent his head towards the papers in front of him. Tavistock, wishing just once that her overactive imagination would take a back seat, pulled the papers towards her and began to read.

Diary of Brenda Skilliton

10th March

Today young Juan came round with some firewood his Dad had cut. I made him some tea and gave him some bannock and jam. We had quite a chat about school and such; when he left he gave me a hug. It was nice to have the company.

Dick came home smelling of drink. He said that the food was burnt and broke the pink vase I won at the fair. Tomorrow he goes to work up at the Callows' farm, he'll be gone for a week thank God.

MIST

11th March

Packed Dick off with a basket of bread and cheese. He gets all his other meals up at the farm with the others. I pity the lambs he brings into the world.

Juan came round after school with a picture of me and I pinned it to the wall. Brightens the place up. I gave him a pie to take round to his Mum as a thankyou for the wood, he seemed pleased and kissed me.

Tonight the house is at peace. I sometimes wish God had blessed me with children but then perhaps it is for the best. I have forgotten what it is like not to listen for footsteps and pray that the drink will have made him sleepy. Sometimes I think the whole of my life has been spent waiting and praying, like walking on eggshells. I have never been able to think of myself. I remember the pink dress my mother bought it for me the first year we were married, I felt like a Queen. I wore it to the New Year's Eve party at that big hotel on the front, pulled down now like all the others. I remember how he said how beautiful I was, the prettiest girl in the world. I was so happy, as happy as when we married. We got home and he tore it in two and smashed most of the wedding presents and then he called me a tart and a whore tramp. I remember him pushing me to the ground with his hands round my neck. He stank of cigarettes and drink, of sweat and dirt. I looked into his eyes. I can still remember the hate blazing there.

The next day, he kissed me and made me my breakfast. He'd put flowers in a vase and cleared away the mess. Mother thought I didn't like the dress and never bought another. That was the last pretty thing I had. I decided it was better not to bother. Funny, I haven't thought of it in years.

12th March

I had breakfast in the garden. I sat on the bench outside and drank milky coffee, the kind he hates. He says I'm so fat that none will have me. Perhaps he is right but I have no energy to find out. The floors need scrubbing and the garden must be dug. I have tried to leave but he always finds me.

Juan brought me a picture of his brother today. We sat outside and he talked about the boats he will be captain of when he is older.

I put flowers on Mother's grave and bought a chop for my tea. I will have it with some fresh mint from the garden, lots of mashed potato

MIST

and some vegetables. I will eat till I am full and then I shall listen to the radio. I have taken it from its hiding place in the shed and it sits on the kitchen table. I am listening to someone talking about the latest films and don't hear the door open. It is him, they have thrown him out and he stinks of drink. He wants money. I tell him it is all gone, that he took all the social gave, and that he will have to wait till tomorrow. He shouts at me and says that I am a greedy lying cow and that I eat it. He throws my plate onto the floor and then he smashes the radio. I see blood on the newly scrubbed wood. It is mine but I do not feel any pain just anger. Anger that I could ever have imagined that I loved him. That I gave up my future for him and defied my parents to do it. That I never allowed the police to press charges the last time. When I lost the only thing I had ever truly loved, the baby.

I remember screaming, I remember looking up. I saw a face at the window small and white. I heard Juan run in. I heard the names Dick called him. Dick turned and went to strike the child, his fist balled like a hammer, the knuckles white. I hit him with the old iron griddle and he turned. Juan picked up a knife from the sink and plunged it into his side and then I hit him till he stopped shouting.

I can remember the peace. I can remember pushing and lifting him into the wheelbarrow. I remember the long walk down the lane and along the old cart track to the farm my parents used to own before they died and he ran it into the ground. He set fire to the house, the home I had loved, to claim on the insurance but he was drunk and they didn't pay up.

We tip him into the old wood shed. Juan still has the knife. He tells me to hold Dick's head and I do. He cuts his throat to make sure and then we cover the body in wood. I padlock the door – no one ever comes here and I will never sell. Now that I can, I dare not; perhaps that will be my punishment.

I stand outside the shed and tremble with the cold and with the knowledge of what I have done and I am relieved. I ought to feel guilt but all I feel is relief. Juan takes my hand and softly says it is our secret.

We go back to the cottage. The barrow I have left in a ditch. It will rust away. I will scrub the floor and Juan will go home to his bed after he has washed.

I remember scrubbing everything, I must have used gallons of water and all the soap in the cottage. It's strange but I feel no guilt or remorse for what has happened to Dick but I do feel an unnamed

MIST

horror over the child's part in it. In the morning I will go to Juan's parents and explain and then I will go to the police. Juan can be kept out of it.

13th March

I have spoken to Juan. He came round this morning to beg me not to say anything. He says that there has been an incident at school and that if there is anything else his parents will send him away. I hold him, his frail body wracked with sobs, and decide for his sake to say nothing. Everyone deserves a second chance. I will go to church and pray. Perhaps there will be an answer there.

20th March

I have reported Dick missing to the police. Most people think he got drunk after the business at the Callows and lay in a ditch and died. Some have said he walked off a cliff and others that he has gone across and won't be back.

People have been so kind. I never realised that he had so few friends, if any; none sober, of that I am certain.

Today was one of the most pleasant yet. I have money in my pocket and the social is due today.

I have found a job at the village school, helping the little ones.

For the first time in many years I am happy.

14th September

The police say they have searched and can find no trace of Dick. They say I ought to presume him dead. I can get help to obtain any monies he might have. I thanked them and walked home rejoicing. All the money we ever had he drank, there is nothing else and even when he was at his worst I would never turn the cottage over to him. It was mine and coward though I was, I had sense enough even then, to not want to be destitute. Besides, a part of me knew that if I handed it over he would leave me.

And now he never can.

Juan comes round every day. At first I looked forward to his visits but something has changed, either I have or he. I do not want him here, reminding me of that evening, cracking secret jokes and watching me slyly from lowered lashes.

MIST

3rd October

Liam has run away, his mother has come to see me frantic with worry.

I tell her that Juan has not visited today as usual. She says that Liam was last seen with Juan near my parents' old farm. My blood runs cold. I go to the hook by the door for my coat and while she is talking to my back, check the keys. There is one missing.

Perhaps they have gone to the beach, I ask.

Her husband, a large, gentle man, arrives, sweat pouring off him, to say that the boys have been seen down on the rocks.

We race to the beach, it is not far over the fields through the gorse. We are all covered in scratches but no one feels them. There is a sense of disaster, a dark foreboding in the air, a heaviness, as of a storm boiling.

I know a shortcut through the rocks and take it.

I round the edge of torn grey slate and feel salt spray on my face. Juan is standing in a deep pool, his hands pressing down on something. I shout and he looks up. In a panic I run to him and grab at the sodden clothes he clutches; they belong to Liam. I see the child's blue face reflected in the water. I know that he is dead before I pull him from the water and lay him on the rocks.

I did it for you, he hisses, he saw me checking, I always check just in case.

We stare at each other and I realise that I don't know him at all. I never did.

Caroline trudged up the staircase, clutching her bottle of Chilean wine. She stopped outside the flat door, uncertain and suddenly shy. What if he expected more than friendship after this meal? The door opened and Paul stood before her, a glass of wine in one hand and a teatowel over the other.

'Long day?' he asked, seeing her pale cheeks and bleak eyes.

Caroline nodded and moved inside, handing over the wine in exchange for the cold glass in his hand. Slowly she sank into the leather sofa and sipped her wine; the smells of garlic and fresh herbs surrounded her and the fire, lit in her honour, turned the room into somewhere safe and oddly reminiscent of childhood.

'Do you remember the parade of steamrollers from the boat to Nobles Park? I watched with my nephew last year. There was a

MIST

solitary Coke can in the road and we saw it squashed slowly by this really big roller from Grimsby. Well, that's how I feel!'

She sniffed, the emotions that had run high all day suddenly erupting in a well of tears.

'Oh, Paul, I don't know if I want to do this any more. Bob says to just put it to one side, like doctors operating, or advocates when they come out of court. That it's just a job, but all I can think about is that poor old lady, nearly blind, terrified out of her wits, tied to something while some bastard cuts her throat.'

Paul moved quickly to sit beside her. He held her gently, his hand stroking her hair as if she were a child. He kissed the top of her head and then her cheek, wet with salt tears. After a little while he handed her a paper tissue and told her firmly to blow.

'Caro, sweetheart, not everybody is like that; most people live and die quietly at home and the most exciting thing they ever see is usually in the papers or on the telly. Just because there's one very sick puppy roaming around out there, doesn't mean to say that everybody else is a potential killer. Look, I'm going to dish up before it spoils. We can sit here with trays on our laps and watch *Eastenders* like an old married couple and if we don't say a word for the next hour, that will make it truly authentic.'

She tried to smile and he laughed, kissing her again, this time softly on the lips.

Five minutes later Caroline found herself calmly eating a large bowl of pasta with some sort of sauce including pine nuts, drinking more wine and wondering what all the fuss had been about.

They watched and commented about the characters of *Eastenders* and then settled into a truly humorous designer show. One designer was thrown into a swimming pool and the other was threatened with the family Rottweiler if he didn't put the lounge back to the comfortable clutter the children had come to expect.

Afterwards they sat and talked. He recounted funny stories about the bank and she shared a few anecdotes concerning her nephew. She told him about how on one memorable visit to Jungleworld her nephew had declared in a loud voice that his best friend's sister was one sexy momma! He was six and she was nearly eight and she hit him so hard he fell down one of the slides headfirst into a ball pool. Afterwards, the little girl spent the rest of the afternoon protecting him from all comers and demanding kisses on a regular basis.

Paul laughed and asked whether that was a hint. She tried to leave at eleven but her heart wasn't in it, and he didn't insist on her going; he just held her hand, turned off the lights and pulled back the duvet.

Mayday

The call came at first light. Bob Callow knew what it was before he picked up the phone. The voice on the other end was young, young and subdued. Quickly he dressed, softly cursing under his breath. He would grab something to eat at the station later, as he thought a full stomach before viewing the scene of crime might be a mistake and eating first would waste time, something he felt he was running out of fast.

The car park outside the old hotel next to Rushen Abbey was almost full, so he parked blocking off a camper van and a couple of bikes. Police officers were already setting up the narrow blockade of tape and a few people living on the other side of the ford were standing outside front doors with cups of tea and dangling cigarettes. A young reporter clutching a small black tape recorder ran towards him, eyes gleaming and hair wet from a recent shower.

'Detective Inspector, can I have a word or two? Is it true that the Mad Druid has struck again?' As he spoke he clicked the machine on and almost thrust it up Bob Callow's nose. Bob carefully moved the machine away from his face and glared balefully at the young man.

'Ah, is that what you're calling him now then? Well, let me tell you this, young Ryan. As soon as we have anything you will be the first to know but as I haven't yet managed to reach the scene of crime, let alone see anything which may or may not interest your readers, I couldn't possibly comment. Now could I?'

The young man's face fell so ludicrously that Bob laughed. 'Look, lad, I'll throw a few bones for the public to chew on after I've seen what's what. Can't say fairer than that, can I?'

'Great, I'll just wait in the car.'

'Good lad.' Bob found himself patting the young man's shoulder

MIST

almost absentmindedly as he walked off, beginning to prepare himself mentally for the next atrocity.

He walked along the river path between trees wreathed in early mist. Bright splashes of violet blue could be seen nestling in patches of early sunlight. He saw rings of silver in amongst the brown water of the swiftly moving stream, as trout rose to the surface, snapping at insects. Further up above the deep black pools he saw movement and light as the arc lamps were turned on. Cameras flashed and he heard the soft tread of wellingtons and plastic covered shoes.

A figure walked towards him, a trail of grey smoke following in his wake.

'Well, Brian?'

'It's another one, Sir, female, middle aged, naked, throat cut, no signs of a struggle and no other evidence apart from the body.'

Bob breathed deeply and marched on. Bodies moved apart as he arrived and he saw with awful clarity the whitened body huddled over the stones of the ancient Monks Well. The head was face down in the water, the hair moving like white snakes. The water still ran a faint pink colour but the spring bubbling through the rocks had already taken most of the blood on its short journey to the stream and then on to the sea.

Bob felt something sag inside. It felt like a hole was forming inside his soul, hardening his heart. One of the scene of crime officers moved the bracken aside, knocking against a limb. The head moved and turned so that Bob saw half a face, the eyes staring.

'Bloody hell! I know her, I'm sure I do! Have you finished with the victim yet? If so, get her out and turn her over.'

Hands pulled the dripping form from the water, the gaping wound livid like an extra mouth. The face was turned to face the light. Bob staggered backwards a few steps.

It was Morag.

Later, when everyone was gone, he sat amongst the ferns and creamy yellow primroses and waited.

Tavistock found him there, hunched over the well like a malignant gargoyle, his hands in the pockets of his coat and his thoughts miles away. Mannanan walked behind her sniffing the air. Something was wrong with the woods around him, something was dogging their footsteps, something alien.

'You called, Sir?'

Tavistock waited for an answer and getting none, drew herself up, put her hands on her hips and gritted her teeth. She wore the expression of outraged motherhood which never failed to get a reaction from her children, usually in the form of a running dive with the words 'it wasn't me' etched in the ether.

'Bob Callow, I have broken several speed limits getting here and I had to bully poor Richard into taking the kids to school. You said it was urgent!'

Bob looked up, his eyes bleak.

'He's killed Morag.'

'Morag!' Tavistock and Mannanan looked at each other.

'Where? How?'

'There.' Bob pointed towards the water bubbling up from the green rimmed depths. 'He walked her up to the well and cut her throat over the springwater.'

Bob shuddered. Somehow this had become very personal and he wasn't sure how he could cope.

Tavistock walked to the edge of the well and leant over. Her foot slipped on wet moss and automatically she put her arms out. Mannanan caught her hand as she fell and something passed between them as their fingers touched. Tavistock had the impression that she was falling and yet her mind stayed where it was, watching as the body fell. A bleak coldness settled round her. She had a new body: old, starved and naked. She found herself looking through another woman's eyes, felt another's pain.

He was holding her head up, his hands tangled in her hair, pulling at the roots; she saw the knife glinting in the moonlight. She couldn't feel her own body; her only fear was that he would taunt her with her death. In her head she held the memories of her family and as she watched the past with almost sightless eyes she recited the Lord's prayer softly. Tears welled as the knife bit into her throat. She looked into his eyes. They shone like blackened coals, completely mad, evil, cold. He thrust her body down, her head plunging into the ice cold water; she could feel the life blood ebbing from her. The cold had woken her. She struggled, frantically fighting against the thought of drowning and she tried desperately hard to scream. The water bubbled up around her and she could feel his naked foot on her head pressing down, the blackness moving in to take her.

'Tavistock, Tavistock, wake up! Come on, love, speak to me. Tavistock!' Bob had seen her fall and had risen as Mannanan reached for her. He heard her scream as she fell.

It was the scream that had frightened him more than any late night horror movie. The scream was one of terror and the voice wasn't hers.

Tavistock struggled against the foot, clawing upwards towards a bright light, and then she heard a voice; it was calling her. The light above faded and as it did the blackness covered her.

'Tavistock, wake up!' Mannanan rocked on his heels above the inert figure and raised his hands to the early morning sun.

As the blackness faded into light she could hear singing. There were monks bent over her. One of them held her head and raised it, lifting her from the water. Gently she was helped to stand; shaking with cold she drank from the wooden bowl they held to her mouth. The water was cold and oddly sweet like honey and violets. The monk who stood beside her pulled back his hood and smiled, his eyes the deep blue of warm oceans.

'You must return to your friends, my dear, they are calling you. And tell our mutual friend that I know he did not break his vows to me. Tell him also that the fool has woken the wolf. He will understand.'

Tavistock shook her head, the vision of light and dark withdrew and the singing voices stopped.

'Tavistock, thank God! What happened, are you all right? Tavistock, if you don't speak to me I'll . . . '

'You'll do what, Bob Callow?'

Tavistock found herself being hugged by both Bob and Mannanan.

MIST

'Now that was truly bizarre. Will you two cut it out?'

Bob lifted her to her feet and looked into her eyes. 'Are you sure you're all right, only for a minute back there . . . ' His voice tailed off. How could he explain that she had been talking with Morag's voice and that Morag had died many hours before.

They began to walk back towards their cars and on the way Tavistock tried to explain what had happened. When she reached the part about the monks she hesitated. Mannanan leant against a tree trunk as she relayed the message she knew somehow was for him.

'He said wolf, you are positive he said wolf.'

'Yes.'

'Who or what is a wolf?' Bob rubbed his cheek. As far as he could gather, he had a maniac running around waking up wolves. Somebody, somewhere, was losing the plot and he had a horrible feeling it was him.

'Did someone say wolf?' an eager voice asked. A figure moved away from the deep shadows of the old monks' bridge and walked towards them. 'You did promise that if I waited? And while I'm here, since when did the police consult writers? Or is this some new policy? Hey, I remember one of the bodies was found in your garden. Is Tavistock Allan the murderer? Is she helping with police enquiries?'

'Ryan.'

'Yes.'

'If you don't put the batteries back in that brain of yours I will personally see that you have a nice early morning bath, a very cold one.'

'And I,' Tavistock announced, 'will hold your feet!'

Ryan looked from one to the other and visibly deflated.

'But if you're a good little boy, I may just give you a few bones to chew on.'

Ryan perked up and turned to follow them down the path, like a lanky Border collie puppy, tape recorder at the ready.

Caroline woke to brilliant sunshine as Paul threw open the curtains. He turned to look at her and went to sit on the side of the bed.

MIST

'Tea,' he said, pointing to the cup resting on the bedside table.
'What time is it?' she asked, beginning to sip the steaming fluid.
'About seven thirty, your office just rang. They want you to go in as soon as possible. Apparently you have to accompany your boss on a bereavement visit, whatever that is?'
'Oh God.'
'What is it?'
'Nothing. Look, I'm really sorry about this.'
Caroline began fumbling for her clothes. Paul smiled, kissed her on the nose and threw a towelling bathrobe at her.
'The water's hot, spare toothbrush in the medicine cupboard.'
'Thanks.' Caroline put on the robe and raced to the bathroom, collecting items of clothing on her way. Her head still felt muggy: the wine she thought, and smiled to herself. The evening had been very different to the one she had planned. Memories stirred and she felt her stomach churn with pleasure. Stop it, she said to herself, and turned on the shower.
Later, as she sat in her car outside police headquarters waiting for Bob and Brian, she felt the first uneasy stirrings of guilt. Her mobile rang insistently; she answered it, keeping a wary eye on the main door.
'It's only me,' the voice said. 'Do you fancy going to the theatre tonight? One of the girls in securities has a part in a play and I promised I'd go. We can grab a curry at the Taj Mahal later, if you like.'
Caroline sighed, guilt slowly seeping away. 'Yes I'd love to. I'll meet you there about quarter to eight. Must go, they are coming out, and thanks.'
'What for?'
'Everything.' She could see Bob turning back to speak to someone inside. Brian stood at his side, balancing his weight from one large foot to the other.
'Must go, bye.'
'Bye.'
She switched the mobile off and started the car just as Bob and Brian reached for the door handles.

MIST

Bob sat in the back staring out of the window while Brian gave instructions for their intended route and filled her in on the latest development.

They were on their way to see Peter, Morag's only child. Bob warned them both to say as little as possible as according to the local police, Peter had nearly collapsed on learning of his mother's death and apparently was still in a tearful state of shock.

They pulled into the curving drive of Peter's house about twenty minutes later and sat in silence regarding a view of cliffs, grey water and wheeling gulls.

The front door opened and a middle aged man emerged. He walked over to the car and they got out, stretching limbs and gathering files.

'Peter Green?' Bob asked, holding out his hand.

The man shook his head and, ignoring the outstretched limb, escorted them towards the front door. 'Peter is waiting inside for you. Please be very gentle with him, he's in a bit of a state.' The man began to turn a large gold signet ring round and round. The podgy finger was red from the constant movement and his face had the blue shading of an incomplete shave.

'Of course; frankly, it's been very good of him to see us so soon,' Bob stated in his most soothing tone of voice.

'Well.' The man paused on the threshold and addressed them almost conspiratorially. 'You see, he had this big fight with his mother about a week ago. He did mean to call round but what with one thing and another. Chef walked out, you see, something to do with turbot, so rude but what can you do? And then Gorgio had a bit of a scene with Fay over the trouble with the linen, not that it was her fault. They should have sent green tablecloths to go with the new menus, but to send salmon pink with yellow.' He stopped and shrugged his shoulders expressively.

'I'm sorry to hear that,' Bob sighed. That's all we need, he thought to himself, guilt ridden relatives on top of everything else. 'I promise we will be as "gentle" as we can but we really do need to talk to Peter. We think his mother knew the killer and so anything he could tell us, anything at all.' Bob stopped, aware that the man in front of him was still muttering about tablecloths and napkins. Caroline and Brian exchanged looks and followed the two men into the house.

The room they were shown into was a large bow-fronted lounge. Loose covered linen sofas and chairs vied for space with a quantity of polished tables and other items of antique furniture. Books were strewn around with Chinese lacquer bowls of pot pourri and dried roses. Peter sat on one of the sofas, wrapped in a large Indian throw of orange and bright azure blue. His eyes were red rimmed and moist with tears, half hidden behind thick tortoiseshell glasses. He looked up and motioned with his hands for them to take a seat. His friend sat down next to him and gently patted his hand.

Bob moved some papers from the armchair nearest to him and settled down into the plump down-filled cushions.

'We are very sorry about having to come round so soon, but we really do need to gather as much information as we can.'

'I'm sorry too, Inspector, I mean Detective Inspector. Mother and I had a bit of a tiff about a week ago; I kept meaning to go round to make it up. And now...' Peter's voice tailed off.

'Yes, they already know, Do you mind if I make some coffee? I'm sure we could all do with one. Won't be a tick.'

'Who?' Bob asked as the friend left.

'That's David, he's my partner, business and, well, personal. We run a restaurant together down at St. Johns, The Mutineer.'

'Oh I've been there, for my brother's fortieth. Very good it was, the food was really excellent.' Brian looked almost excited and both Caroline and Bob shared surprised looks.

'What did you have?' Peter asked, almost animated.

'The stuffed crab with Pernod and the brill with sorrel butter; oh, and the triple chocolate parfait.'

'Very good choice. The brill is difficult to get but it's one of my signature dishes.' Peter almost preened and looked for one moment just like a large gaudy peacock parading his tailfeathers. Bob coughed and cleared his throat.

'Right, well, perhaps you could tell us why you had a row with your mother and when you last either saw or spoke to her.'

Peter looked from one to the other and began to plait the ends of the large ornate gold tassels which appeared on nearly all of the cushions he was surrounded by. 'Well,' he began uneasily his eyes shifting from the fireplace to the door and back again.

'It was about the tablets.'

'Tablets?'

'Yes, she made these tablets, sort of herbal sleeping pills. Only...' His voice tailed off again as David re-entered carrying a wicker tray containing a large ornate gold cafetière and assorted white bone china coffee cups and saucers. He put the tray down and began to pour and hand round the small delicate cups.

Bob sipped cautiously and sighed. 'Excellent!' he announced, as he broadly beamed at David who almost blushed with pleasure. Peter, watching them, gave a slight petulant toss of the head and continued.

'The thing is, according to a friend in London, the stuff she made up when mixed with alcohol acts a bit like that date rape stuff the police are so anxious to stop. You must know the kind of dope I'm talking about; it's been on national TV, for God's sake.' He paused and took a gulp of coffee. 'I told Mother she should stop making them; I mean, just think if someone got hold of some and, well, used it for his or her own purposes. Of course, Mother went off the deep end, called me a few things I'd rather not repeat and slammed the phone down.'

'Bingo!' muttered Bob under his breath.

'Sorry?'

'Oh nothing. You don't happen to know what these pills were made of or who she gave them to?'

'No, but I do know she wrote down all the names and addresses of the people she supplied. It was just in case there were any side effects, or their doctor had prescribed something which might have clashed.'

'This was some sort of book?'

'No, one of those big box files. She kept it in the kitchen with the kitchen scales. I'm afraid it was all on loose-leaf paper. Mother wasn't really that organised.'

'I see. Well, I expect we will come across it when we go through her things. Did she by any chance have a dog?'

'Yes, a sort of terrier called Tabitha, the original hound from hell; imagine Victor Meldrew only two foot long with sharp yellow teeth. Why?'

'We think that the person who killed your mother may have killed the dog as well. I don't suppose you have the name of the dog's vet?'

'I think she used the young chap out at Ballasalla, you know, the practice just past the railway station on the way to the airport. Name of Smith or it might have been Jones. Mother just referred to him as Andrew. I know she took her to have her nails trimmed about three weeks ago because she wanted me to take them in the car. Needless to say I didn't. It's a nearly new Merc with cream leather interior. I mean, just imagine what that mutt could do to it. It takes at least twenty minutes to drive there from her house.'

'Yes, I can sympathise. Did your mother have any other relatives or close friends she might have talked to during the last week or so? She has a granddaughter, I believe.'

'Shona, she lives with her mother, my ex-wife, in Castletown. Number four Harrison Avenue, off Penrose Hill. Another reason why Mother and I were not that close, in case you're wondering.'

The bitter note in his voice made Brian look up from his notebook. David coughed meaningfully and Peter smiled thinly. 'I'm sorry, this has all been a bit of a shock and, well, to be honest I'm really not looking forward to the inevitable meeting with my ex at the funeral. We didn't part on exactly the best of terms and Shona hardly ever talks to me.'

'That bitch has a lot to answer for and of course, the whole thing will be my fault!' David got up as he spoke and went to stand by the window, his hand gently resting on Peter's shoulder for a moment.

'Is that it, Inspector?'

'For now yes. I understand that your mother's friend Mr Williams has already identified the body?'

'I asked him to. I can't stand hospitals and, well, places like that.'

MIST

'I see,' said Bob, carefully placing the empty cup on the small gilded table next to him. 'Thank you for all your help.'

David rose as they did and said, 'I'll see you out.' He followed them to the front door and as they drove away Bob could still see him hovering in the doorway, a dark shadow at his side.

2nd May

The honourable member for Sodor North stared out of his murky office window and sighed. Today was yet another Tuesday, the day when Tynwald, one of the oldest governments in the world, met and discussed issues raised by other members of the house and sometimes by the media or members of the public. He knew that there would be more than one enquiry as to the recent spate of murders and as he was Minister in charge of law and order he was being held by some to be more responsible than the killer himself. He knew that this morning would make the night of the long knives look like the annual Hospice teddy bears picnic and that the enemies he had made on the way up would be shod in their best boots to kick him on the way down. He sighed again, pushing a piece of lank hair from his eyes. His meeting with the Chief Constable the previous day had done nothing except confirm that the killer was still around, something the press already knew, as shown by their ambushing him before he'd even set foot in his office earlier that morning.

He ground his teeth in remembrance. Not only had that young idiot from the local paper been lurking outside his front door but so had a camera crew from Border News, several members of the English and foreign paparazzi and practically every freelance journalist on the Island. He glanced at the clock. Five minutes to go. He just had time for a quick black coffee and to go over the question papers again.

'And if,' he muttered to himself, 'they ever catch the bastard, he'll never come to trial because I shall personally strangle the bugger with my bare hands!'

The Chief Constable was at the same time thinking on the same

MIST

lines, except he was all for pouring concrete over the Mad Druid during the building of the new Douglas bypass and access road.

There was a knock on the door. 'Come in!' he bellowed.

Bob poked his head round the door, the rest of him following cautiously behind.

'You wanted to see me, Sir?'

'Yes, I did. Sit down, Bob. Tea? Coffee?'

'Coffee, please, Sir, strong, black and dripping in sugar.'

The Chief Constable smiled almost sympathetically and moved over to a sideboard covered by an assortment of books and files, where the coffee machine lurked, quietly bubbling like a malignant cauldron. After a few minutes he returned bearing two Douglas 2000 mugs.

'So, how are things progressing? I believe that you have received several leads, which I trust are being chased up?'

'Yes, Sir. We believe the perpetrator is one Juan Moss. We've managed to dig up most of his records before he and his family moved off Island about thirty years ago. He was, according to various school reports, a very bright, some might say extremely bright, child; however, he had few friends and according to his old headmaster, now retired, was generally shunned. There was apparently an unfortunate incident with the school's hamster.' Bob paused, judiciously tasting the coffee, which he had to admit was surprisingly good.

'Bring my own in, safer.' The Chief Constable almost smiled at Bob's appreciation and opening the top drawer of his desk produced a tin of shortbread. Carefully passing a yellow, sugar dusted finger of biscuit to Bob, he asked, 'You said hamster?'

'He was found by one of the teachers torturing it with a cocktail stick. The poor creature died shortly afterwards and a request was sent to the DHSS for an assessment to be made regarding the family. The head also told me that he was in the process of contacting the parents to have Juan sent to another school but then the unfortunate incident with the younger brother occurred and they moved.'

'And this incident, did it have something to do with Juan?'

'We believe so, yes. His brother died, he was four. The official report says that he met his death by accidentally falling into a deep rock pool.'

'And the unofficial report?'

'That his brother pushed his head under the water until he stopped breathing!'

'I see.'

'There was one other thing. Apparently this child of eight also assisted in the murder of one Dick Skilliton. He then helped dispose of the body and the reason he gave for killing the brother was because the brother had seen the older boy checking up on the corpse.'

'Good God! And can this witness identify this Juan Moss?'

'Not exactly; she was the first victim.'

'Damn.'

'We do have a diary which sets out the first murder and the drowning of the little boy, if we can prove that the Druid is this Juan Moss.'

'What happened to the family after they moved?'

'We tracked them to an address in Manchester where they died.'

'Convenient.'

'Yes, we think so too. Unfortunately they died in a fire caused by, as far as the local fire service could ascertain, a discarded cigarette. The three bodies were identified by means of dental records and the coroner recorded a verdict of accidental death.'

'All three?'

'The two adults were definitely identified but unfortunately young Juan hadn't actually been to a dentist except for the usual check and clean so we can't be absolutely certain it was him.'

'I see, and if it wasn't?'

'If it wasn't, we have fairly good grounds for suspecting that we have murders numbers three, four and five. Unfortunately at this late stage we have no way of knowing what happened. We've checked with Greater Manchester CID. The remains of the house were pulled down by the council shortly afterwards, to make way for some road widening exercise. We've checked Juan's old school records and we can't, as yet, find any trace of a missing school friend or other missing lad of about the right age and description.'

'Any chance you could dig something up if you went over there?'

'Logic dictates that it's too old a story but...'

'Go on.'

'I just have this feeling that there might be something. If I could talk to some of his old teachers and friends of the parents.'

'Right, off you go. Take a week if necessary, find something, something I can keep the bloody politicians quiet with, and Bob, try and do it as cheaply as possible.'

'Yes, Sir, and if the lead goes on to somewhere else?'

'Follow it up. The TT starts shortly and we have to have something by then or we'll both be doing traffic duty at Windy Corner for two weeks!'

Bob grinned and stood up. The Chief Constable raised himself from his round leather chair and moved to stare out of the window. He sighed and turned, fixing Bob Callow with a pair of almost black gimlet eyes.

'I want this little bastard, Bob. I don't care how you do it, just do it.'

Bob nodded and moved towards the door. The audience was over. It had gone better than expected. At least he still had a job. Whether his wife, Moira, was going to be best pleased was another matter.

3rd May

Bob sat behind the large, slow moving tipper truck and swore. The bus had been bad enough as it crawled from Douglas to Ballasalla, stopping at all points in between, but at least he had managed to pass the damn thing on the straight past the Mount Murray. What he wouldn't give for a nice blue flashing light and a very loud siren. He looked at the digital timepiece in front of him and swore again. He had ten minutes to check in, including finding somewhere to park, preferably under a large shrub. The last time he'd flown across he'd forgotten. Overnight, summer had arrived and he still had the burn marks from his plastic seats and the metal tipped safety belt, which he'd sat on, to prove it.

He began to edge out just as he passed the Fairy Bridge, being careful to say hello to the fairies in as pleasant as tone as possible. He needed all the help he could get, even theirs. Not that he believed in the little malignant buggers. Mind you, he thought, as he saw no traffic on the other side and stepped on the accelerator, he didn't believe in dead gods either and he seemed to spend a fair amount of time consulting one.

The tipper truck driver began to speed up as Bob passed him. Their eyes met as Bob passed the cab window and the driver made an anatomical gesture at Bob's receding bumper. Bob had one, little known, talent and that was an uncanny knack of remembering number plates, a talent he'd acquired as a bored schoolboy at a country bus stop.

'I'll have you later, my son. You'll keep!' thought Bob happily as he screeched up the hill towards Blackboards and hit ninety as he cleared the first bend.

Now all he had to do was break every single speed limit between the Whitestone and the airport and he was home and dry. He took the milkfloat on the wrong side of the traffic island causing palpitations to an old wrinkly, in a bright yellow mini. He could still see the little car squatting in its stunned and stationary position half way round the roundabout.

He was going to do it!

Three minutes later he was parked, wedged between a very large dark green shrub and a smart black Mercedes. He legged it across the car park and a taxi blared angrily as he raced across the double zebra crossing, coat flapping and head bent for maximum wind resistance.

He had the tickets in his hand as he launched himself at the check-in desk.

'Have they made the final call?' he anxiously asked, handing over the tickets.

'Where are you travelling to, Sir?' the young lady replied, answering his question with another.

'Manchester,' he said, his voice edging towards a scream. Another voice inside his head danced up and down like the White Rabbit whilst chanting, I'm late, I'm late, I'm late.

'Passengers are due to board shortly,' she said before commencing the routine list of questions concerning the packing and carrying of luggage.

Bob answered, a bead of sweat wobbling on his forehead before being wiped hastily away. The rabbit continued to chant and the sense of time running out increased. He almost grabbed the boarding card and his hand luggage, a moth eaten black sports bag, and ran to the departure area. He hurled himself up the escalator past the over-large fairy lights and towards security.

Whilst his boarding card was checked, two of the security staff recognised him and grinned.

'Where's the fire, Bob?' asked the more elderly of the two, as Bob threw all the bits of metal from his pockets into what looked suspiciously like the little hospital trays for kidneys and other necessary organs.

The other younger man morosely checked his bag, pointing out, as he handed it over, that he didn't know anyone read the *Beano* any longer.

MIST

'Very funny,' muttered Bob as he collected his things and raced towards gate three. No one was waiting at the gate and nobody was collecting boarding cards.

Defeated he sank onto a waiting chair and stared morosely out of the window.

'Good morning, ladies and gentlemen. Manx Airlines regrets to inform all passengers waiting for JE321 to Manchester that this flight has been delayed due to technical difficulties. We do apologise for the delay and will advise you further as soon as possible.'

'Bugger!' said Bob.

'Coffee, black,' said a voice above him. He looked up to find Tavistock standing over him with two white plastic mugs of coffee in her hand.

'Thought you'd missed it, huh?'

'No, well, maybe just by a second or two.'

'Liar!'

'Anyway, what are you doing here?' Bob sniffed the brownish liquid in front of him and sipped cautiously. It did, admittedly, taste vaguely of coffee.

'Book signing in Manchester, followed by one in Newcastle and I'm going to a film première.'

'Posh frocks, prawns on toast and even bigger prawns in dinner jackets?'

'No, a film made by local kids with the help of the Prince's Trust. You remember Roger, I introduced you to him at the Empress last October, runs a drama club with able and disabled kids.'

'Roger? Not the little guy with the clipboard, never stopped talking. Told me all about the crimes perpetrated by that youth gang? Boss, wasn't it?'

'That's the one. You said it wouldn't happen on your patch because you'd feed 'em to the crabs in bite sized pieces!'

'Nice chap. Offered to show me round the Venerable Bede's place.'

'Church.'

'Really?'

MIST

'Yes.'
'Bet he put me down as a born again Liberal!'
'I think "Fascist Pig" was the term used.'
'Told you we got on. Oh well, send him my regards, won't you.'
'So, what do you reckon the delay is?'
'The wheels fell off?'
'All the clever money's on bunnies on the track!'
'That's a new one.'
'Bob?'
'Yes, kiddo?'
'Any news on our mutual madman?'
'Charming way to address the old and venerable, I must say!'
'Tell me he isn't here, please tell me he isn't.' Bob turned towards the source of the voice. Mannanan sat on the blue velour seat next to them, eyes twinkling.

'How the hell did you get here?' Bob asked, staring at him. Tavistock coughed and shrugged her shoulders.

'In your car, I've been driven by her before, so I thought I'd try a more sedate pace for a change. Did you really have to use that sort of language; that poor man was only doing his job. After all, the whole point of having a rural bus service is so that it can pick people up and let them off again and the wretched fellow has to stop to do it.'

'What every 500 yards!'
'If necessary.'
'Stop it, both of you, people are beginning to think we've had a tiff!' Tavistock said glancing anxiously around.
'I don't mind if you don't. Give us a kiss and they'll stop looking.'
'Bob.'
'Yes, love?'
'Get a life.'

Tavistock's mobile pinged somewhere in her bag, and when found chirruped crossly like a newborn baby with wind.

'Yes,' she said 'What? ... No, it's in the fridge, under the fromage frais ... I don't care, he's not having tuna and peanut butter ... Not unless you want to drive them home with the window open ...

MIST

Because he made such a mess last time... Under the stairs in the red book bag... yes he did, because I spent an hour sorting it out... Don't forget Emily's cookery money; it's fifty pence... Because I will not buy them anything at all!... Love you too, see you Wednesday night... Give my regards to Mother and for God's sake don't let Father anywhere near the fish or he'll sauté them in garlic butter. Do you know how much the average Koi carp costs these days? Richard, sweetheart, they aren't ours and when Chris gets back from Kenya he will expect to see his award winning pets alive and well and not in the throws of being recycled by our offspring and my potty old man... Yes dear... Me too... Bye.'

'Last minute debrief, huh?' Bob finished his coffee and began to wonder about risking the raspberry Danish.

'Good morning, ladies and gentlemen. This announcement is for all passengers travelling on Manx Airlines flight JE321 to Manchester. This flight is now ready for boarding. For your comfort we will be boarding this flight today by seat numbers. Could we ask passengers seated in rows 8 to 17 only please to come forward now to gate number three for boarding. We apologise for any inconvenience caused by this delay which was due to technical problems and we wish you a pleasant flight. Thank you.'

'At last,' Bob sighed, gathering up his belongings.

Together they moved towards the gate and eventually onto the plane where they discovered, to the amusement of Mannanan, that they were sitting together. The unoccupied seat in between was then taken up with their coats, papers and one large interested minor deity.

Bob, settling his bulk into the seat, murmured his appreciation of the fact that they were travelling on the somewhat larger 146 rather than the usual bus-like ATP. Tavistock shrugged. As far as she was concerned the extra space was very welcome and she would rather not spend time on the reason why.

'Voices off,' mused Tavistock, as they heard childish voices raised in a heated debate over who would get the seat with the window. They could hear the dulcet tones of the air stewardess trying to calm them down, eventually managed with the bribe of being able

MIST

to have a handful of sweets from the pre-flight sweet basket, instead of the allotted one sweet per person.

'You know what the really great thing about kids is?' she asked Bob.

'Nope,' he replied as he hunted for the in-flight magazine in the pocket in front of him.

'Occasionally, when you don't have them for a bit, the whole world seems different. Do you know I can expect to go the whole day without being slimed. I can read a book in peace and drink hot coffee without interruptions.' Tavistock smiled to herself and stretched, cat-like. 'I can even eat chocolate without being surrounded by three pairs of starving eyes!'

'Ah, the joys of parenthood. Glad mine are both safely packed off to University. Wonderful thing, higher education. Mind, we still worry about them but we don't have to do anything about it. Parenting by phone is much better than shouting verbal abuse across the hall. Not that I ever did, of course.' He coughed and began flicking through the magazine on his lap.

Tavistock looked out of the window at dark tarmac and a distant view of King William's College.

'Penny for them?' Bob asked watching her.

'What?' Tavistock turned, Mannanan had somehow merged with the coats and was almost invisible. Faint sounds of snoring emanated from his chair which both Bob and Tavistock were trying studiously to avoid noticing.

'You look tired.'

'Oh well, I am a bit. Haven't been sleeping all that well.'

'Ah.'

'I have these dreams.'

'Dreams about what? Oh, thanks, love.' Bob reached into the proffered basket of humbugs and leered at the waiting air hostess; somehow he managed to take two. The air stewardess then leant over the spare seat to hand the sweets to Tavistock and Mannanan awoke to find himself almost nose to nipple with a pair of ample breasts. He chuckled and Bob, turning to see what was happening, choked on his sweet.

MIST

'Serves you right,' Tavistock muttered as she watched the aircrew going through the motions of a safety demonstration.

'You were saying?'

'I have this dream about being caught in a room. There are bodies trying to crawl along the floor, only they don't have any faces, just red masks with eyeholes, then I smell smoke and the room explodes.'

'Go on, and then what?'

'Nothing, I wake up, why? Bob, you look like you've seen a ghost?'

'I think you ought to read this.'

From the brown leather document wallet beside him he extracted several sheets of paper and after a quick check handed one to Tavistock. Mannanan glared at them both as Bob leant over him to pass the paper across. Disgruntled at being disturbed he shuffled uneasily before disappearing again.

Tavistock read the paper and looked up at Bob. She was visibly shaken by what she was reading and swore quietly. By now the engines had sprung into life, flaps wiggled on the wings and the plane began to taxi along the runway where it turned and stopped.

The seat beside them muttered about hating this bit and that if God had meant man to fly he'd have given them hollow bones. Bob and Tavistock both hissed 'shut up' as the plane raced along the runway and finally pulled sharply up into the clouds.

'You ever have odd dreams before?' Bob asked. Tavistock's face was white and he'd begun to notice the dark circles under her eyes. The plane shuddered as it shook itself free of the dark clouds below and began to race over a golden sea of cumulus. The sky was a brilliant blue, trailing bands of high cirrus like Christmas angel hair.

'When I was little, before we moved to the Island, we had this house in Tunbridge Wells. It was one of those old Victorian villas near Grosvenor Park. One night my grandmother came to stay while my parents were out at some dinner. I must have been about three years old but I can't remember much except for the dream, if that's what it was. Grandma heard scraping noises along the hall and found me standing on a chair trying to peer through the glass

MIST

top of the bathroom door. I told her I wanted to go to the toilet but the man wouldn't let me in.'

'What man?'

'That's what my Grandma said, so I told her it was the nasty man who was holding the lady's head under the water in the bath. Well, she opened the door and showed me there was no one there, gave me a hot milky drink and tucked me up in bed.'

'And then what happened?'

'All hell broke lose when my parents came home to find Grandma wandering around with a bottle of Guinness and a copy of the Bible. About a week after that she came round and had a huge row with my parents.'

'Why?' Bob asked.

'She'd gone round to see the vicar and some guy from the local historical society and discovered that the house had been rented by a local doctor who had allegedly married several women who had signed away their dowries to him and had then died peacefully in their sleep. At least that's what the death certificates said.'

'But surely someone would have become suspicious?'

'Not necessarily; the servants never stayed very long, the wives were fairly similar in that, according to several friends of his wives, they had no near living relatives and were all known to be both timid and physically weak. The word used was consumptive but that could have meant anything. Apart from which the man was a doctor, a good one and people trusted him.'

'So what happened?'

'One of the neighbours heard screaming one night. The following day the doctor reported that his good lady had died of heart failure during the night. The police became suspicious and he stood trial. They found marks round the victim's neck and other bruises but they had no other proof. Later he was acquitted and moved away to live in Brighton.'

'Good God! And I thought our justice system was bad.'

'There was a final postscript to the tale. This doctor then remarried a local girl whose long lost brother arrived suddenly from New Zealand to find his sister the recipient of a large scrapbook containing news cuttings from the local papers giving lurid details of the trial. Nobody knew where this book had come from; they presumed it was from a friend of one of the previous victims. Big brother then took matters into his own hands and removed his sister from under the alleged murderer's roof. A month later our friendly GP was run over by a brewer's cart; funnily enough, according to the police it looked like the cart had run over the body a couple of times before the horse was quietened down.'

'Really?'

'And, guess where the last wife's family dosh came from?'

'The local brewery?'

'No, but you're close. They had shares in five or six large hotels and guest houses in various seaside resorts and the local brewery had a very close and highly profitable relationship with them all.'

'And your dream?'

'If it was a dream, stopped the moment we moved. My parents, after finding out the truth, had the bathroom altered and removed all the old fittings but I still had the dreams and then started to sleepwalk round the house locking all the doors. I even managed to lock my father out when he'd gone to get some coal; the poor man had to climb through the ventilator window in the larder. We are talking damp basement, dead of night, teddy bear pyjamas, very old dressing gown, soggy slippers and interested police constable with large torch. Dad had a lot of explaining to do!'

'So dreaming about the odd psycho is nothing new then?'

'Not really, except that now they don't feel like dreams and they are in colour.'

'That's because they're not dreams,' Mannanan muttered, gradually emerging from the folds of cloth.

'Breakfast?' the stewardess asked, saving Bob from a rather terse reply.

Hungrily they both unwrapped their rolls and Danish. Bob had his usual trouble with the foil lid on the orange juice. Exasperated, Tavistock grabbed the plastic cup and, with dark mutterings, expertly opened it and gave it back.

'Thanks,' said Bob, tucking into his croissant.

'What do you mean by not dreams?' Tavistock asked, smearing butter on her roll.

'What I said. You, my dear, have the sight and what you see is the past. Sometimes just flashes as at the well and sometimes whole sections of time.'

'Hang on a minute; do you mean to say that she could go somewhere and actually see what had happened years before,' Bob asked, an idea forming in his head.

'That depends.'

'On what?'

'On whether or not she has a trigger to start off with.'

'Such as?'

'Being in a room which contains strong emotions, for example the bathroom where the wives were drowned. Or by touching something which had been in possession of the victim or murderer.'

'So the other morning by the well?'

'You touched the stones when you fell, the same stones the victim lay on as her life blood drained away.'

'He really does have a way with words, doesn't he? Coffee thanks, black.' The air stewardess gave them both a slightly strained smile and then departed to sort out the two small children in the back row, who were now having a very vocal discussion over who owned the last leg of the Three Legs of Man mint.

The plane began to slow and began the descent into Manchester. Bob and Tavistock watched as the wings emerged from damp clouds and began to circle the fields and houses below.

Between them Mannanan began to fidget. 'I hate this bit even more than the last bit; something's bound to fall off; what happens if we run out of fuel?'

'We glide softly into the nearest golf clubhouse or sandy bunker, depending on the pilot's handicap. Just go back to sleep,' said Tavistock.

Green fields and houses spun past the windows as the plane dipped and then banked sharply to the left. Mannanan groaned and the plane came into land, engines whined and airbrakes screamed as the large metal cylinder ground to a halt.

MIST

After waiting for the doors to be opened and the steps to be lowered to the ground they finally left the plane. They then scrambled aboard the waiting bus which insisted on taking the long way round to travel the one thousand yards to the terminal. Mannanan had refused point blank to enter another metal tube and walked from the now silent plane to the terminal entrance. Bob and Tavistock could both clearly see him as the bus meandered past the waiting planes and airport vehicles, a tall brown figure, arms folded, scowling horribly at everything around him.

After collecting their luggage, they split up: Tavistock in one taxi to her signing and Bob in another to his meeting with Greg Mathews of Greater Manchester CID.

Bob rubbed his eyes, trying to make some sort of sense of the assorted papers in front of him. The litterbin at the side of the desk was full to overflowing with polystyrene cups and biscuit wrappers. Greg Mathews sat across the desk, arms folded and a thoughtful expression on his face.

'So you lot out there,' he said in the tone of voice that made Bob think of the X-Files, only he was no Moulder, 'think that this eight-year-old, Juan Moss, killed his parents and some other poor sod and then disappeared without trace, assuming some other identity, and nobody has yet twigged at all, with the possible exception of two or three people who are now dead.'

'Got it in one, give the lad a cracker!'

Greg grinned. He and Bob had originally met at Police training college, where they had become almost unbeatable when it came to snooker and drinking. Later, despite joining two very different forces, marriage, and children they had remained close friends. Greg attended Bob's marriage to Moira some twenty odd years ago and Bob and Moira had attended Greg's, all three of them. Greg's first wife died in a car crash on the M6 two years after the wedding; on the rebound and only a year after the funeral he married his deceased wife's younger sister. The divorce followed amicably enough two years later. Finally at the age of forty two he met a tax inspector called Clarissa. It was love at first audit. Three years down

MIST

the line he was the proud father of two and happier, Bob thought, than anybody with young children should be.

Bob stretched and rose from the table; he felt tired and yet a part of him was sure that sitting somewhere in the jumble of papers was a significant piece of information and that they were both missing it entirely.

Greg sat back in his chair, arms clasped behind his head, and stared at the ceiling.

'To be honest Bob, I've been through all the records I can find which could have any bearing to the period in question and I've come up with absolutely nothing new.'

'No missing lads of around the same age?'

'Nope, none that stayed missing. There were a couple of possibles who turned up elsewhere.'

Bob's nose twitched and a shiver of something ran down his spine. 'Such as?'

'Thing is, none of them had any sort of association with this Juan Moss and believe me, I've checked schools, mutual friends, clubs and even medical centres. Nothing.'

'Any crimes since then which haven't been solved with the same modus?'

'Nope.' Greg scratched his chin thoughtfully. 'All of the possibles have been accounted for, even the ones that have been in and out of the prison system both here and abroad. None of them appear to have any connection with our lad here.'

'The thing that gets me is that you don't suddenly appear on a small island as a fully fledged murderer. There has to have been some sort of apprenticeship. Perpetrators like that don't just happen and somewhere along the line he must have made mistakes.'

'You really are convinced that he's alive, eh?'

'Positive.'

'A feeling in your water?'

'Something like that. Speaking of which, mine's a pint, your shout.'

Bob moved towards the door and the coathanger which swung precariously from a small plastic hook stuck on the wooden panel with what looked to him suspiciously like Blutack. Slowly he shrugged himself into his new jacket and turned back towards the papers on the desk.

'What?' Greg asked, noting the frown.

'You know, I'm sure there's something I've missed and it's staring me in the face.'

'Come on, we've been at it for hours. What you need is a bit of fresh air and a decent drink. After that I'm taking you to a place that does the best pies on the planet or I wouldn't have married the cook. You can even have a go on Jack's new Playstation.'

'This would be the small bald chap in the laundry basket?'

'That's my boy.'

'He must be all of six months!'

'Nine, it's an old photo.'

'And very advanced for his age?'

'I'm looking after it, for when he grows into it. Besides, it's one of the perks of being a more mature father, you have more time to play with their toys!'

Bob laughed and shook his head. He was still chuckling as they left the building and walked towards the Red Bull public house. This was a squat red brick building which sat, glaring malignantly, on the corner of two main roads. Traffic sat bumper to bumper as what appeared to be the entire population of the Isle of Man tried to get home. As the cars passed he glanced through the windows to see faces universally grey and resigned.

Children glared at him from a jeep long enough to make rude Maori-like gestures before resuming hostilities. The woman driver appeared deaf and dumb to the conflict in the back as she sat hunched over the wheel, teeth set in a permanent snarl.

Bob was reminded vividly of Tavistock curled over the wheel of her car as they spun on corners and lurched over cattle grids to get to the second scene of crime at Druidale. It seemed years ago now and he still appeared to be no nearer to learning the new identity of Juan Moss. He sighed. Greg watched him thoughtfully and instead of going into the pub walked straight past towards an off licence further on. Bob looked briefly at the door of the public house and as he did a gaggle of young lads surged out of it, clutching at each other's shoulders and arms whilst singing something vaguely familiar. The dirge was in at least four different keys which was odd as there were only three of them.

'One must be a ventriloquist,' Greg muttered, uncannily reading Bob's thoughts.

'You used to do that a lot.'

'What?'

'Working out what I was going to say before I said it! The only other person who can do it is Moira.'

'Ah well, just goes to show what good mates we were, eh?'

'It was bloody annoying, if you must know!'

'Kept old Sergeant Mills on his toes though. Do you remember that stake-out at Appleby Junction?'

'How could one forget? Soggy chips and one bucket. I've had better facilities in a Mirror dinghy on a gravel pit!'

'Those were the days. Thank God I'm too old and past it now. At least a desk has heating and hot and cold running constables, including one who has a mum that makes a Victoria sponge with a filling at least three inches deep.' Greg sighed and stopped in front of a large green and black painted glass door. A sign stuck on the inside informed them that they would accept all known credit cards and currencies, some of which Bob had never heard of.

'Here we are. What do you fancy, red or white?' Greg asked, opening the door.

The door clanged shut as they entered the premises. Interesting boxes were heaped in corners bearing hand written descriptions of vineyard grape and recommended food.

Bob felt his mouth watering and was dragged towards the counter but not before he'd managed to fill both arms with assorted bottles.

'You're only staying for dinner!' Greg hissed.

'Evaporation,' Bob whispered, digging around for his Switch card. 'Besides which, some of these were on that food and drink programme and could I get hold of a bottle? Nope, not even for a week's blind-eye parking. Moira's going to be dead chuffed when she sees this lot.'

'Oh, so what are we having?'
'Bottle of Barbara d'Alba. Bit pricey but a very nice Italian red, estate bottled. You'll really like this.'
'Do you still brew your own?'
'Not since the boiler incident.'
'Boiler incident?' The young lad on the other side of the counter stopped packing the bottles into a cardboard carrying box, leant on the counter and blatantly listened.

'I made this batch of blackberry and left one of the demijohns on the shelf near the boiler, just overnight. When we walked in the next morning it had exploded up the wall and all over the radiator. Moira and the kids had only just finished redecorating. You would not believe the mess.'

'Oh yes I can. I still remember that batch of apricot exploding in the airing cupboard when we shared that flat in Liverpool.'

'That wasn't the reason why I stopped. It wasn't just the mess.'

'Go on.' The young lad leant nearer; the silver ring hanging wart-like from his left eyebrow twitched obscenely.

'Well, when we tried to wipe it off, the paint came off too.'
'Bloody Nora,' said Greg.
'Streuth,' said the lad.
'So what did you do then?'
'Used the rest of the wine as paint stripper and ate humble pie for a month. Actually, it's quite funny now but at the time Moira was literally spitting nails, she was that cross.'

'My dad used to make his own. He mixed up this fruit punch for my eighteenth; I think it was a couple of bottles of peach wine and lemonade.' The lad pensively stroked stubble. 'It were that strong, one of my mates tried to do a Batman impersonation off a railway footbridge on the way home. Took four of my other mates to get him down. Missed the express by minutes.'

'People don't really appreciate the home-made stuff like they used to and that's a fact; ah well.' Bob sighed wistfully, pocketed his card and picked up the box with its precious load.

Later at Greg's house after helping to bath two small children and the usual ritual of foiling the two-year-old's escape bids, Bob found

MIST

himself seated round a small table in the kitchen before a gigantic helping of steak and kidney pie with onion mash and something green. It was delicious.

Meanwhile, in another part of Manchester, Tavistock Allan was coming to the end of a long and rather trying book-signing session. It was late night shopping and the bookshop in question had insisted that she stay late, thereby giving as many people as possible the opportunity of having one of her books signed but only after they had of course spent the required £5.99 to purchase Tavistock's latest paperback. A lot of people had turned up, mostly to ask a variety of questions varying from the inquisitive to the blatantly insulting.

One elderly lady had demanded, in a sharp falsetto which carried a surprisingly long way, whether she felt ashamed by the amount of blatant violence she included in her books, especially towards children. As Tavistock had never killed any small children off she was understandably puzzled, that is until the young woman standing next to the querulous old biddy quietly told her aunt that Tavistock was not Ruth Rendell. Apparently satisfied, the old woman toddled off to the back of the shop, returning ten minutes later with five of Tavistock's books which she insisted were all signed and dedicated to various relatives and friends. Tavistock gritted her teeth and smiled in a friendly fashion, despite the old lady's barbed comments about the state of her handwriting and the fact that she was scrawling away in Biro and not ink!

Finally the ordeal was over. Her wrists hurt from writing and her throat had dried completely. Her legs felt thick and heavy from sitting down too long and every muscle in her face ached.

Politely she thanked the remaining members of staff, made a mental note to send a dead rat in a cardboard box on a spring to her publisher and managed to leave quietly by the back entrance.

Later she sat in the only comfortable chair in her hotel room, her aching feet propped up on two cool, cotton clad pillows and a small table. On the windowsill sat a large steak sandwich and a bottle of red wine. Traffic purred and shunted below and a constant current

MIST

of chip-scented air scurried under the pale lace nets which fell in soft scoops around the bow fronted aperture. In one hand she held *Busman's Honeymoon* by Dorothy L. Sayers and in the other a half full glass of wine. As soon as she had returned to her room she had kicked off her shoes and run a hot deep foaming bath. Every muscle sank gratefully into the hot water and afterwards, draped in a large cotton bathrobe thoughtfully provided with the compliments of the management, she had rung room service and then rearranged the furniture.

The children had rung to say goodnight. Richard had still not been able to find the cheese grater and the Koi carp remained uncooked. Tavistock had long since realised that her husband was not a naturally domestic creature and that as long as food wasn't actually moving he would attempt to eat almost anything. It had taken some time for her to realise that he never read packets so best-before dates were less than useless. Hairy green plant life could be cut off cheese and bread which would then be toasted and there was no such thing as a preheated oven. All in all the best solution seemed to be the temporary installation of her father who loved to cook and her mother who would restore the kitchen to almost hospital cleanliness afterwards.

Loving endearments were uttered by all, even her father. Normally he would find at least three things that needed to be put right, from the electrical wiring in the spare room to the proliferation of dandelions in the lawn. Tavistock wondered whether he had discovered something so awful that it couldn't even be discussed over the phone. Tentatively she broached the subject with her mother, who after consideration decided it must have had more to do with helping George build a Viking longship and thereby not having any spare time for anything else. Tavistock shuddered inwardly as the vision of what possibly awaited her on the lawn swum in front of her eyes. Final loving endearments were made by all and it was almost with a feeling of relief that she had put the phone back on its plastic cradle.

Time passed quietly. She felt a pang of guilt which was very vague and lasted all of three seconds. She sat up and listened. She had had peace, a bath uninterrupted by screeching infants determined to share her water, a meal not cooked by herself and best of all no housework. She could, if she wanted, leave wet towels all over the bathroom floor and clothes and books all over her bed and the surrounding carpet because just for tonight it was somebody else's problem.

At about eleven thirty the phone beside the bed rang, short trill bursts of irritated sound. She snatched up the phone and barked into it. If it was Richard asking her to find one more household item she would hang him up by his tie in the wardrobe for at least a week, or make him go to a lecture on Jacobean Literature. He'd been surprisingly well behaved for weeks after the last one she'd dragged him to.

'Yes!'

'Is that Mrs Allan?'

'Why?'

'There's a policeman downstairs who says he has an appointment.'

'Oh.'

'I've made him show me his warrant card; it does say he's a policeman but . . . ' The voice faded, doubt echoing down the line.

'But?'

'Well, he rattles.'

There was the sound of mutterings and a voice sharply demanding that the git with the acne give him the phone.

'Bob?' Tavistock shouted. 'Is that you?'

There was a distant 'Yes' and more muttering.

'Oh just send him up. He's an old schoolfriend and mostly harmless.' The phone was disconnected and Tavistock went to the door. She peered out cautiously so that she could let him in without anybody else being disturbed. She could see the headlines now: 'Evening raid on popular novelist.' Richard would be overjoyed!

Bob emerged from the lift and clanked towards her, tie slightly askew and his grey raincoat almost off one shoulder at a youthfully rakish angle. She moved to one side as he wafted in, a distinct aroma of garlic and wine following in his wake.

'What did you mean by saying I was mostly harmless?' he asked as he carefully navigated his way towards the chairs at the end of the room.

'Nothing. Oh God, you do rattle!' she exclaimed, shutting the door and taking his coat before it fell off.

'Thanks, love,' Bob muttered as he eased himself into the one comfortable chair next to the window.

'I don't mind having my own things littering the floor but I'm blowed if I have maidservice clearing up yours as well.'

'What did I do?' Bob looked at her like a puppy that had just been trodden on. It was the same look Richard always wore when, on several occasions, he had arrived home to bear the brunt of his children's major crimes against the state and in particular their less than understanding mother.

'What do you want?'

'Ah well, I had this idea and . . . is he about?'

'Who?'

'Him. You remember: long brown tunic, very see-through, hates planes.'

'Haven't seen him since we left the airport.'

'Oh.'

'Why?'

'I had this idea!'

'At this time of night and in your present state I'd put money on it involving undergarments and traffic cones.'

Bob's eyebrows shot upwards like demented caterpillar's. 'How can you say a thing like that about a member of Her Majesty's finest? I'm hurt deeply.'

'Bob, I have known you since we both made our first plasticine models of Odin's Raven. I've even, God help me, spent a week with you under canvas at Glastonbury, so please don't say another word. Just have a coffee, sober up and find your own hotel!'

Bob sighed. 'Oh thou of little faith and low opinions. Why don't you just get dressed and I can tell you all about it in the taxi.'

'What taxi?'

'The one I'm going to order while you change. Mind if I leave these here?'

MIST

Tavistock watched in mute fascination as Bob began to remove bottles of wine from the voluminous folds of coat and jacket.

'Big pockets,' he said, grinning broadly.

Tavistock gave up. Knowing Bob as she did, he would stay there until she did get changed or, even worse, offer to help. She grabbed things from drawers and banged the wardrobe door shut. Bob studiously ignored her. Sighing dramatically, she shuffled into the bathroom and noisily locked the door.

They got out of the taxi and looked around. Bob rummaged in his pockets for change and discovering only Manx coinage reluctantly had to offer up a crisp ten pound note. The cabdriver sighed and in turn quickly counted out the change, all the while looking around for any sign of trouble, reminding Tavistock of an elderly meerkat.

'What about a receipt?' Bob asked, pocketing the change.

'Bog off!' was the reply as the taxi shot off. The sound of gears being brutally misused shrilly screeched in the soft night air, as the taxi driver hastily turned and sped back towards the city centre.

Bob and Tavistock stood silently watching the receding tail lights as the night settled around them.

'I still think that this is quite possibly one of the strangest ideas you have ever had!' muttered Tavistock. 'The house isn't even there any more; it's part of a municipal park, for God's sake, probably being used at this very moment by a vast collection of druggies, glue sniffers and mixed fornicators.'

'This from the woman who had a sheep as a sex object in her last book!'

'It was done with taste. I was nominated for an award, I'll have you know.'

'Don't care, it was still crap.'

Tavistock, choosing to ignore the remark, continued her uneasy scan of the neighbourhood and asked, her voice almost a whisper, 'Where are we going?'

Bob began extracting objects from various pockets. One appeared to be a small slim torch and the other a thin folded piece of paper.

MIST

With a certain degree of care, due in no small part to a slight problem with hand and eye coodination, the paper was unfolded.

'Well, according to this map from Records, we first find the end of Ferret Street and then walk about two hundred yards in an easterly direction. Hence the use of one trusty compass which I pinched this evening.' Bob grinned, apparently more than satisfied with his minor sortie into the criminal world of petty theft. Tavistock sighed. Bob carried blithely on. 'If we do that correctly, we should, all things being equal, arrive at the start of Carter Road. The Moss family lived at number four.'

Bob moved off, coat flapping in the light breeze, and Tavistock trailed behind him, furtively looking to right and left. A figure detached itself from behind a bush and approached cautiously.

'What the hell is he up to?'

'Who?' Startled, Tavistock leapt to one side, hands slicing the air as her defence class instructor had advised.

'Bob. I'm Greg, by the way, and you must be that writer he goes on about.'

'Are you the bloke he trained with, the one with the passion for cacti and Ford Corvettes?'

'Got it in one.'

'Do they train you all in how to creep up behind people and frighten the living daylights out of them?'

'We like to call it "moving in on a suspect in an unobtrusive manner". Scaring them shitless is a bonus.'

'I suppose every job has to have its own peculiar little perks. There is one thing that bothers me though: just why are you here? And now we're on the subject, just how did you get here?'

Greg stopped and scratched the back of his neck in a thoughtful fashion which had never failed to irritate his wife. 'I saw him stealing, or rather borrowing, my son's Action Man compass so naturally, feeling curious, I followed his taxi here. To be honest, when he stopped at your hotel I got really puzzled, decided to hang about a bit and lo, he departs hurriedly with you in tow and ends up in this Godforsaken hole. You wouldn't mind telling me why?'

MIST

Tavistock gave him a sideways look and was about to explain when Greg suddenly asked, 'What on earth is he doing now?'

Greg and Tavistock stopped and stared at Bob who now appeared to be doing some sort of dance. After about a minute of frenetic capering, he launched himself onto the ground and started scrabbling about on the grass.

Tavistock looked around. They seemed to be in the centre of a patch of lawn, surrounded by low bushes and a few stunted alder trees. Overhead a concrete bridge carried fast moving cars and other vehicles to and from central Manchester. In the silence of the park, the roar of traffic appeared louder and their current position a lot lonelier.

'Bob, what the Alan Titchmarsh are you doing?' Tavistock hissed.

'Dropped the bloody compass, didn't I,' Bob replied, his voice lowered to that of a whisper, all the while searching frantically in the damp turf, inadequately assisted by the light of a small pencil torch.

'Is he all right?' asked a fourth voice.

'That you?' Tavistock asked, squinting uncertainly into the distance. The surrounding area appearing to mist over as she spoke. Greg took a step back, almost walking through the figure of Mannanan.

'Yes,' Mannanan answered, shimmering in and out of focus to reappear just behind Bob's crawling shadow.

'Who?' Greg turned to her, trying to work out who she was talking to. When it appeared that Bob was also conversing with the same patch of air from a kneeling position, he began to wonder about the amount of alcohol they had all consumed.

With a worried frown he began to back slowly towards the road. The crack of broken wood sounded loudly in the open space, causing Bob to turn towards him.

'Greg,' Bob hoarsely whispered, 'what are you doing here?'

'I could say the same of you. Why are we all whispering; there's nobody else here?'

'Greg, old thing.'

'Yes?'

MIST

'Remember when we were working on that kidnapping in Tatswood, oh, years ago.'

'Yes.'

'Do you recall that daft old biddy who finally found the pipe the kid had been stuffed in.'

'The smelly psychic? Had a passion for cheese and raw onion sandwiches.'

'That's the one.'

'Why?'

'Tavistock here can do the same sort of thing.'

Tavistock was about to demur when Bob trod heavily on her foot. She gave a muffled yelp and swore. Greg looked from one to the other, uncertain as to his sanity or theirs.

'The thing is,' Bob continued, 'if we could go back in time and find out what really happened twenty five odd years ago, we might have more of an idea about how young Juan managed to disappear and whether or not he's still alive. If he died in the fire then we have a load of unfortunate coincidences but if he didn't we have a very accomplished murderer. We also have a very experienced one. One that not only knows how to cover his tracks but also to move elsewhere afterwards.'

'And just how do you reckon we can go back in time? Hold a séance and talk to the dear departed!' Tavistock asked sarcastically.

Greg felt a shiver run down his spine. Mist was creeping along the grass, the air around growing colder. For some reason he could feel the presence of a fourth being; normally he would have laughed the feeling off but he couldn't. Beginning to feel increasingly and illogically frightened he moved closer to Tavistock.

'It might be possible.' Mannanan considered, stroking his chin. 'But we would need to be standing in exactly the right spot, Tavistock would have to be in physical contact with something from that time and you need three living beings to form the triangle.'

'Good.' Bob almost sighed with relief. 'This is, I reckon, the front room of the house. I also have in my pocket a small piece of charred remains purloined from records and Greg makes living being

MIST

number three.' Bob grabbed Greg's hand as he spoke in a vicelike grip and passed a small plastic bag over to Tavistock with his free hand. Greg yelped with pain and shock. Tavistock gingerly opened the bag containing what looked at first glance like a piece of charcoal and at an encouraging nod from Bob held it in her hand. Finally, she held Greg's hand with her free hand. As she did Greg started, eyes dilated as he finally realised he could see the person both Bob and Tavistock had been conversing with. The realisation shot through him as if he had just had a bucket of iced water tipped over him. Suddenly sober, he clutched the hands holding his and tried to calm the steadily rising panic he could feel crushing his chest.

Bob, realising that somehow Greg could either see or sense what was happening, nodded at Mannanan. They then simultaneously clasped Tavistock's hand, the one that held the smoke blackened lump of bone.

Mannanan stood in the centre of the group, head bowed. Slowly he began to mutter in a strange language. The words sounded oddly musical and as the words grew, so too did the mist until it surrounded them on all sides. The air felt dank and chill. The sounds of traffic overhead ceased, blotted out, as if they had never existed.

Greg watched in horrified fascination as the ground beneath him appeared to swell and then dropped sharply until he realised that he was floating about six inches above what appeared to be a cheap flower patterned rug.

Walls began to grow around them, covered in a red and white print of tea-roses with grey ears of wheat, entwined snakelike amongst the pale foliage. Ugly, deep red velvet curtains limply hung in front of tired nets which in turn did their best to hide a bow window of peeling paint and brown fungus infected wood. All three living watchers then realised almost simultaneously that they could neither speak nor move. All independent thought processes had ceased; all they could in fact do was see.

A man sat in an armchair nearest the closed lounge door. He was smoking and drinking from a can of beer. The act of inhalation was

MIST

followed immediately by the loud gulping of brown froth. A woman sat on a worn sagging sofa and slowly knitted, pale rods of plastic stabbing like knives at the purple and pink striped wool. Occasionally she looked up to watch the comedy on the television, her laugh bordering on the manic. A wooden coffee table stood in front of her, its surface covered in matching orange and brown ceramic tiles, the grout nicotine-stained and uneven. On the one remaining chair hunched the figure of a boy staring intently at the television screen whilst nervously biting his fingernails.

The door opened and a second boy entered. He was dressed in clothes similar to the boy in the chair and he carried a tray laden with tea things. With great care he placed the tray on the coffee table.

The woman smiled, her eyes nervous. Tea was poured. Each person, except the second boy who carefully shielded his cup from view, drank. The man remarked that it had a faintly odd taste and the woman rounded on him, sharply reminding him of the beer he had just drunk. Still thirsty, he drained a second cup, as did the woman and the boy in the chair. The second boy then placed his untouched cup back down upon the tray. Carefully he collected up the cups, informing the group that he would wash them up. Noiselessly he left the room.

Gradually the occupants of the room began to succumb to sleep. One by one, heavy eyelids closed and the room became silent except for the canned laughter from the television and the carefully timed ticking of a gold coloured carriage clock upon the mantelpiece.

After a while the second boy returned, his face shaded by the dull light and by a curtain of lank hair framing his face. At times it almost appeared as if he wore a crude stocking mask which appeared to shift as he moved around the room. Carefully he removed a cigarette as it fell from the man's numbed fingers, stubbing it out in the empty beer can.

He talked as he slit the foam in the cushions bolstering the woman's body. His eyes glinted and he smiled as he told her unlistening form that he had taken the new bottle of Valium she had hidden that morning in the bathroom cabinet.

MIST

He took hold of the other boy's legs and dragged him to the window. Carefully he turned him round and rearranged the boy's arms, to look as if he had tried to crawl to the window. The boy slept on, saliva dribbling from the corner of his mouth, slack and ruby red. Juan watched him lying on the floor, his body rising and falling gently. Carefully he removed the boy's belt and slowly pulled the torn and patched trousers from around the pink young flesh. Then he removed his own clothes, piling them neatly against the vacant armchair. The man stirred, heavy eyes trying to open. Juan went to him. He stood over the man and spoke, choosing his words with care.

'Father, I know you can hear me and I know you can see me. So watch me now with my friend here.' He pointed calmly to the body on the floor. 'Trev usually does this in the back of cars and up against the urine soaked walls of white-tiled toilets. I know because I've watched.' As he spoke he knelt down and calmly pushing the young boy's legs up, bending them at the knees, he entered him from behind. His father, desperately fighting against the drug-induced immobility, sat in the chair, choking noises issuing from his throat.

The boy began to moan faintly as Juan finished. Juan looked down on him and laughed, His voice had an unpleasant edge to it, the sound of visciousness only just held under control. He wiped himself on a piece of discarded cloth and moved back to his father.

'So here we are, one big happy family. We live together, sleep together and die together. A tragic accident, caused by a casually dropped cigarette. A lesson to be learned. The Moss family united at last by death, only I will go on. I know you've always hated me. Well, guess what: it was mutual. Only I've done something about it.' The man moved slightly and Juan bent his head down so that their lips almost met. 'What's that? Let Mother go? Oh no, we couldn't have that now, could we? Besides she really died when her "baby" died. After all, that's why she needs the pills, so she doesn't have to face the truth. The truth being that I killed her darling baby boy, and you know what?' He paused, his voice, low, edged in

MIST

cunning. 'I enjoyed every last minute of it.' The man's eyes finally closed, his face a purple mask of fury that he couldn't release.

Carefully the boy closed all the windows and drew the curtains. He dressed carefully before returning to his father's chair where he removed a cigarette from the discarded packet, lit it and, drawing in deep breaths, exhaled with a satisfaction which was almost sexual. Casually he dropped the glowing cigarette into the folds of foam. He kissed his mother with nicotine stained lips and walked from the room, closing the door softly behind him. At first nothing happened. The television chattered on, the clock on the mantelpiece ticked and the occupants slept.

Slowly black smoke seemed to fall to the floor, crawling along the ground like a living thing, rank and deadly. A red tongue flickered amongst the folds of chintz, darting amongst the thin material, as if a nest of snakes had hatched and were hunting their first kill. Suddenly, a ball of fire flashed and rushed towards the ceiling, spilling out and stretching to catch curtains and trailing nylon net which melted in poisonous shreds and globules. The air thickened, flames reaching out and taking hold. With a roar the television exploded. No sound now but the ever growing orange light turning white at its centre of origin and the faint whine of a fire engine. The occupants, long dead, heard and felt nothing.

Walls became opaque as the watchers clearly viewed the surrounding crowd of neighbours. Every face registered shock and horror in varying degrees. Every face except one. That solitary visage smiled slyly, half hidden by a dark grey hood. Almost as if he sensed their presence Juan Moss straightened up, shouldering the heavy backpack he carried. Then, without a backward glance, he turned and walked away out of sight.

Slowly the orange light faded as the fire died down, the walls melted into mist and the ground again reached their feet. Hands white from holding on released their grip and the watchers universally fell upon the grass, gasping as if out of breath.

Overhead the dawn broke, tearing aside grey clouds in a sudden dazzle of pinks and golds.

4th May

Unable to sleep and frightened that if he did he would relive the horror of the night, Bob found himself wandering the early morning streets of Manchester. Finally exhaustion and hunger forced him into a small steamy corner cafe, every table but one occupied by members of the building trade and associated professions. He slumped into the empty seat and stared unseeing at the greasy plastic-covered menu. A woman, large and smelling faintly of violets, came to rest beside him like a large tanker coming into dock.

'Well, ducks, what will it be? The breakfast special or something else?'

Bob looked up, eyes red from lack of sleep. The woman smiled sympathetically and gently removed the menu from his hands.

'The special it is and a nice pot of tea. You look like you could use it.' With a laugh she turned and sailed off towards the counter shouting out the order of one special and a large tea as she went.

After what seemed only a few minutes she returned bearing a large brown plastic tray on which stood a fearsome looking blue china teapot, a white mug and a small stainless steel jug of milk. 'Sugar's on the table,' she stated, placing each item carefully in front of Bob's bemused gaze. 'And don't you pour it straight out neither, let it brew or it'll be nowt but gnats' piss,' she admonished as she departed to the sage nodding of heads on either side of Bob's table.

Bob after waiting a suitable length of time or at least until his ministering angel had departed to confer with a rather portly skinhead at the end table, poured himself a large mug of what looked suspiciously like creosote. Convinced that the teapot like most of its kind would dribble everywhere but in the mug, he held

MIST

it gingerly in both hands as if it were an unexploded bomb. Tea slunk effortlessly into the mug and Bob, slightly bemused, added milk and sugar. As he was cautiously sipping, his 'special' arrived. It was, he had to admit, very special: a cholesterol addict's wet dream. The plate was the size designated 'large dinner' and was almost entirely covered by food. Two large sausages snuggled up nicely next to three rashers of crisp bacon, two golden soft-yoked fried eggs, round fried potatoes, mushrooms, one tomato halved, two slices of fried black pudding and a crisp golden triangle of fried bread.

Bob swallowed and stared at the plate in front of him, the only thought in his head being that if Moira ever found out he'd be on a low fat veggie diet for at least a month.

'Toast is coming,' announced the woman beside him.

Bob looked up, eyes wide and red rimmed. 'But I can't eat all that!' he exclaimed.

'Oh yes you can, ducks, and you're not leaving until you do. Right lads?' Again the silent chorus of nodding heads. Bob sighed; he knew defeat when it hit him, besides which the smell wafting up and attacking his nasal hairs was making his mouth drool. Slowly he picked up the knife and fork beside the plate and made the first incision. Egg flowed across perfect whites and fastened around the potato rounds, as Bob lifted the first forkful to his lips.

Later he sat back and pushed the empty plate away. Blood sugar had been restored, the world was a wonderful place and his faith in his fellow men and indeed women had been restored.

After paying the bill and adding a tip, which the woman had pocketed with a smile, he set forth to find a florist.

The idea of visiting the grave of the Moss family had come to him between the ingesting of the final piece of sausage and black pudding. He had phoned Greg at home and had purchased a large bunch of spring flowers and now he stood on the corner of a quiet residential street awaiting his lift. Several people passed and commented on the flowers, including a couple of youths, heavily body pierced, who informed him that Viagra must be a wonderful thing for olds like himself. Resisting the urge to beat them around

MIST

the ears with the daffodils in his hand he smiled sweetly and informed them that 'at least he was old enough to know how'. Greg arriving at that moment and, summing up the situation before parking on the kerb with a squeal of brakes, wafted his warrant card at them.

'Get in,' Greg barked, pushing open the passenger door with his free hand. 'This isn't the Isle of Man, you know; you don't banter with the average youth: you either read 'em their rights or keep well away.'

'Well, in that case I'm glad I do live on an Island even with the occasional vacationing psycho in residence. At least when some yob spits at us it makes the front page!'

Greg said nothing as he pulled away from the kerb and drove to the family Moss's last resting place.

He parked alongside the cemetery wall as near to the black iron gates as possible.

'This is it, plot 259; according to the verger it's near a big bent yew and a bench.'

'You're not coming then?' Bob asked.

'Nope, I've had my fill of that particular family, thank you, and I expect I will still be having lurid nightmares for years to come.' Greg picked up a tabloid newspaper from the floor between the driver's and the passenger seat and buried his head in it.

'Right,' said Bob. 'I'll just pay my respects and totter back here then.'

'Good.'

'Fine.'

Bob climbed out of the car, opened the gate and after consulting the rudimentary plan affixed to a post at the apex of paths which looped and snaked off in most directions, hastened off towards plot 259.

Ten minutes later Bob found himself standing in front of the gravestone donated by a collection of neighbours which marked the spot under which the late family Moss had been buried. It was overgrown and unloved, the stone itself smeared with graffiti and lichen. Almost reverently he placed the small bouquet of flowers on

MIST

the kerbstone facing the grave and looked out across the cemetery to the hills beyond. He was about to turn when he felt the air stiffen; the hairs on the back of his neck bristled and he felt something standing behind him. Fear gripped him, a cold horror working its way into his lungs.

It was then that he heard the sound of voices as if a group were talking some yards off. Each voice had the hissing sound of a venomous snake.

'He was evil from the moment he was born, born bad he was.'

Bob started at the words; a bead of perspiration gleamed in the morning sun, before he wiped it away with his hand.

'He took my baby, but I wouldn't listen. I knew, I've always known, but I wouldn't listen.'

Bob tried to turn, but his body failed to obey. He felt as if he was welded to the spot, rooted like a tree, too terrified to turn round but unable to run away. Overhead a black crow flapped past, its shadow reflected in the gravestones as it passed.

'He said he was my friend. My friend. Friends don't do what he did to me, do they?'

Bob tried to speak but only a strangled croak came out. The presence moved nearer, the air cooling as it approached. In front of him the yew tree bent and waved in the bright spring sunshine, rays of light dappling the dark ground underneath.

'From the first time I looked into those eyes, I knew. Oh yes, I knew. I should have burnt him with the afterbirth. I wanted to. Oh yes, I wanted to, and that bastard, that hell's spawn knew.'

Bob swallowed. He could feel them growing nearer, stronger, each voice taking on the character of the living. Grass rippled at his feet, gentle waves of green. And all around the air thickened, heavy as if waiting for a storm to break.

'I never loved him, not really. When he was little I couldn't even bear to feed him. Was it my fault?'

Bob braced himself against the anger in the air, emotion so strong he knew that if he could only reach out a hand he would be able to touch it.

'I loved him, really loved him. Let him do things to me, shameful

MIST

things, because I loved him.' The voice broke then, unable to continue.

Bob felt the sigh settle around him; a faint draught as of butterfly wings fanned his face.

'May he rot in Hell!'

'He was born bad.'

'He stole my name, you know. That's all he wanted. Just my name. Not my love.'

Bob stirred. Here it was then, the reason why they had come to him but could he ask the question he knew he had to ask? There was silence broken only by the sound of wind, leaves and a solitary thrush singing its tiny heart out.

He licked his lips. He could feel saliva flowing again, moistening his mouth, his tongue no longer glued to the inside of his mouth. Finally he managed to ask, his voice a tight whisper.

'What is your name?'

The stone in front of him began to shimmer as if the sun was warm enough to heat the air around in order to produce a faint haze. Over the name 'Juan Moss' another emerged, the new letters raised over the old:

TREVOR MULATTO

The air beside him moved and he felt them all leaning towards him. Words spilled out of the air, dark and heavy with barely suppressed menace. A smell like sulphur assailed his nostrils, making him want to sneeze and gag at the same time. Words of hate eddied around him, the anger that they still felt, cold and keen like a knife blade, sharpened over many years. Without warning the headstone cracked, splitting in two halves. A scream, the sound of a thousand pieces of chalk scraping against slate, pierced the air; a faint shower of stone dust floated upwards. Bob felt them closing in and willed his body to move. At last he could feel muscles and bone move at his command and he began to run as though pursued by demons, his heart hammering within his chest as if he were running from the gates of Hell itself.

Slowly the discarded flowers began to scatter. The headstone

MIST

stood intact, the tired stone still retaining its original inscription as the soft blooms brushed against it, blown about almost playfully by the wind.

Tavistock made her solitary way to the railway station, still nervy from the previous night. She found herself starting at every noise and shadow and so it was with a certain amount of relief that she clambered aboard the waiting train to Newcastle.

She sought a vacant seat with a table and after depositing her luggage beside her settled back to wait for the refreshment trolley. When it finally arrived, wheels squealing like pot-bellied pigs, she bought a coffee. Throwing caution to the wind she added both of the packets of sugar that the smartly dressed young man had handed her.

Leaning back, she sipped the hot sweet fluid and watched trees, fields and houses roll past the window. The scene outside blurred from brown to green to grey as she crossed the backbone of England rushing headlong to meet the North Sea. Something, some intuition, told her that many years before Juan Moss had travelled this way too.

Meanwhile Greg and Bob sat in the interview room and stared at the ceiling.

Finally Greg spoke, breaking the silence.

'The Mulatto nose, that poor kid had the nose; I thought I'd recognised the face.'

'What?'

'The Mulatto nose, a nose feared and revered by the lower strata of life frequenting certain glory holes in the nether regions of our fair city. You know, I think it's about time to have a little chat, off the record, with old Daddy Mulatto.'

Bob remained seated, deep in thought, until Greg slapped him on the back and shouted, 'You coming or what?' as he made his way to the door.

They tracked Daddy Mulatto down to the inner sanctum of a seedy club hidden in one of Manchester's less salubrious side streets,

MIST

backing onto Manchester's Victoria station. The club straddled the first floor of an old Victorian terrace of shops, containing a boutique, a travel agent and a Spar supermarket.

The room was ill lit and stale; the smell of old tobacco and beer hung suspended in the air. They were ushered in by a middle aged cleaner, still clutching a mop and bucket, a limp cigarette dangling from thin, carmine-tinted lips.

Bob looked across the room and realised with a start, that the reason why Daddy Mulatto was so named owed nothing to Italian tendencies but everything to the fact that he was the dead spit of 'Big Daddy' the wrestler, the man who had frightened and amused generations of wrestling fans including Bob and his two children, both boys fans almost from birth.

Daddy Mulatto beckoned them in, motioning them to take a seat, his face giving nothing away.

Greg sat in the chair nearest the desk, while Bob lounged against an old wooden mantelpiece supporting a motley collection of books and ledgers including what looked like a fairly comprehensive collection of Tolley's Tax.

'So, to what do I owe this rather dubious but unexpected pleasure?' asked Daddy Mulatto in a deep bass voice.

'You ever heard of a lad called Trevor Mulatto?' asked Greg.

'Why, what's he done?'

'Nothing, he's dead.'

'Don't surprise me. That side of the family got forgotten way back.'

'Why?' Bob asked, suddenly interested. Daddy Mulatto didn't look the type to disinherit over anything less than full scale mass murder and even then he'd probably find some kind of mitigating circumstances.

'Drew a knife on Ma, didn't he?'

'Who?' Bob and Greg enquired in unison.

'What's with the bleedin Greek chorus? Trevor's dad, of course, my brother Mickey. Knew he'd gone off with some poor cow and that there was a son. So he died, did he? I presume we ain't talking natural causes.'

MIST

'He was murdered by a lad called Juan Moss. The press call him the Mad Druid of the Isle of Man. Or at least we believe he was,' Bob added, seeing the anxious look Greg had thrown him.

'Oh, so when was this? I'll send some flowers.'

'Bit late for that now. He died about twenty five years ago. I can give you the grave number if you like.'

'What!' Daddy Mulatto looked genuinely startled and leant forward to stare into Greg's eyes. 'You sure?'

'Positive,' both Greg and Bob assured him.

'Again the Greek chorus. Pity Music Hall died, regular Flanagan and Allan you two are.' Thoughtfully he sucked in his cheeks. 'That figures, makes sense considering. Been bothering me for a while but then again, none of my business.'

'What's not your business?'

'Ma died couple of years back, so I thought I'd look the lad up. Mickey got knifed in some club down south. Deserved it by all accounts; after all it might be legal but still I don't hold with shirtlifters, especially not ones who like very young meat. That's why he went for Ma. She found out about his tendencies, wanted it sorted out before the nipper was born. Anyway, to cut a long story short I tracked the lad down to some bank in South Shields. Went in there and asked to see him.' He stopped talking and began hunting in his desk for something.

'And?' Greg prompted.

'Weren't him, was it.' Daddy Mulatto grunted with relief and handed them two photographs. One, brown tinted, was of a young boy of about six clutching a dirty teddy. 'See the nose? And this is one I took of the other guy and hey presto, no nose!'

The other picture was of a man in his early thirties. Bob grabbed it and peered closely.

'Did he know that you'd taken this?'

'Dunno. Telephoto lens other side of the street, upper window.'

'Mind if I borrow this and let my team back home have a look?'

'Be my guest. So tell me, how did my nephew die?'

Bob and Greg exchanged glances. 'Are you really sure you want to know?' asked Greg.

MIST

'Yes.' Daddy Mulatto folded his arms and waited.

So Greg told him, hesitantly at first and then as he went on, the story poured out from him, lucid and graphically descriptive.

The big man sat and listened and at the end he rose and moved to the one small, grime-encrusted window. A pencil he held in his hand snapped loudly as he turned back towards them. His eyes glistened and his voice sounded rough and unsteady.

'You must be pretty sure of yourselves to tell me this?'

'You could say that, yes,' Greg replied, praying that he wouldn't ask either of them just exactly how they had acquired this information. It had been difficult enough explaining to himself what had happened and he'd been there.

'You don't happen to remember anything else about this impostor? Anything at all?' Bob asked.

'Well yes, as a matter of fact, I kept tabs on him through some lads up north that I have, let's say, a certain agreement with.'

'And...'

'Shortly after my visit he left the bank and disappeared, sold his flat and moved. The estate agent reckoned he'd got a transfer. And that was that. I can screw money out of a bank but not information. I'll write down the branch address if it helps.'

'Please.' Bob stared at the photograph of the face of the man they knew was Juan Moss and frowned. There was something he should remember. Daddy Mulatto finished writing and handed a sheet of paper over to them, the writing neat and legible.

'Don't look so surprised, Greg lad. I've even got one of them Open University degrees, in accountancy.' He stood up, pushing the leather swivel chair back against the wall and walked to the door which he opened for them. As they passed he placed a large paw-like hand on Bob's shoulder and leant down to whisper in his ear.

'I don't know you, but I have a feeling you'll catch this bastard and when you do, I want to know before it gets into the papers. You understand what I'm saying.'

Bob nodded, now anxious to leave and start the inevitable paperchase of enquiries.

MIST

They left and as they turned towards the stairwell they could still sense Daddy Mulatto standing in the doorway, waiting.

5th May

Bob sat in front of the telephone and willed it to ring. Greg entered the small interview room which seemed even smaller now, owing to the reams and boxes of records and assorted faxes and computer print-outs.

'So this is what happens to the rainforest,' said Greg, looking around for a clean space to put down the two dripping mugs he held.

'Is that coffee?' Bob asked.

'Could be but then I've always been an optimistic kind of sod. So who are you waiting for?' Greg motioned with his head in the direction of the silent telephone.

'The personnel department of the Island bank. We've tracked him down to their International division and guess what, he's changed his name – by deed poll.'

'Not surprising if you'd murdered one of the Mulattos and big Daddy showed up. You'd change your name too.'

The telephone rang and Bob grinned as he picked it up, the grin fading fast as he realised it wasn't the bank but his Department.

'Brian? Oh you did, did you ... Missing? ... For how long? ... well, find out ... Yes, Paul Stone ... *What?* ... Yes, *now*.'

The phone was slammed back down and Bob sat in stunned silence,

'Tell me.'

'Greg, I'll tell you on the way to the airport.' As Bob rose, quickly gathering up pens, paper and his jacket tossed over a chair, the phone rang. He answered it and listened. The conversation was brief and at the end of it Bob sighed and, thanking the person on the other end, deposited the phone back on its stand almost in slow motion.

'Bad news?'

MIST

'You could say that. Paul Stone, alias Trevor Mulatto, alias Juan Moss, alias the Mad Druid, rang his branch manager this morning and quit. To make matters even more interesting, Constable Brian Clague, who incidentally buggered off as soon as the photo of said Mad Druid arrived on his desk, has now returned with the interesting information that not only is one of my team going out with the aforementioned nutter and has been for the last month or so but she has, surprise, surprise, vanished from the face of the earth. Now you tell me, why didn't the silly sod just say, "Gosh that looks like Caroline's boyfriend!" Maybe then we could have had a chance of grabbing the bugger.'

'Ah.'

'Ah, indeed! Apparently young Caroline saw the photo when it first arrived hot off the fax, screamed, "But he was with me all night," grabbed her handbag and did a runner. Did the little idiots let me know? Did they hell! Instead Brian goes off tilting at windmills and no one any the wiser. That mad bastard's had over twelve hours to kill Caroline and leave the Island. The age of the headless chicken is here. How in God's name am I going to explain this to the Boss?'

'Come on.'

'Where are we going?'

'A small green runway, where a friend of mine has a little plane all juiced up and raring to go. Or he will have by the time we get there.' As he spoke Greg pulled out his mobile and began punching numbers.

They arrived at Barton airfield, secreted just outside Manchester, within what felt to Bob like minutes. Brake drums glowed red, the smell of hot metal following in the car's wake as it slewed to a halt and Greg cut the engine. A man walked quickly towards them in the slightly superior way that all pilots seem to have and stopped in front of the car. Greg got out, as did Bob, shaken and most distinctly stirred. Hands were shaken as Greg introduced the pilot as Joe, an old friend and golf partner.

Joe began to explain about flight plans and weather, all the time walking towards a small white and red plane, black leather flight bag swinging against his legs.

'This is it.' Joe said, climbing onto the wing and opening the perspex hatch. 'Just stick to standing on the black bits when climbing up,' he admonished, pointing down at the wing treads.

'Very nice,' Bob muttered. He'd been in bigger hatchbacks. Uncertainly he looked at Greg who grinned and pointed at his watch.

'Time is being lost, Bob.'

Bob gingerly climbed in and settled himself in the seat next to Joe. The hatch was clipped shut and checked, Air Traffic consulted, and before he'd even thought to wave goodbye, he was being helped into life jacket, seat belt and a pair of large grey radio headphones.

Bob listened to the almost coded radio messages as Joe conversed with the air traffic controller. Each switch was checked, each dial consulted; at last, satisfied, Joe started the engine. The large single propeller whirred as the little plane juddered towards the runway.

'Ready?' Joe asked as he carefully made a final check on the assortment of buttons, dials and knobs on the dashboard in front of them.

'Ready,' Bob muttered, swallowing.

'Right, here we go.'

The little plane rushed forward. Joe pulled the stick up and the plane shot like a cork from a bottle and soared into the air. Roads, fields and trees flattened as they climbed steeply upwards. Wisps of grey cloud tugged playfully at white wings as the little plane banked and turned towards the Isle of Man. Bob looked about him at the immensity of the sky and then down towards the quilt of grey-green and felt something almost like joy.

'What sort of plane is this?'

'Robin.'

'Not a Reliant?'

'No.' Joe smiled, amused. 'Although it does have three wheels.'

'You mean which came first, the Reliant or the Robin?'

Bob watched as the ground below gave way to a green and white expanse of the Irish Sea which stretched out towards the grey ridge

MIST

of cloud hugging the distant horizon. Small boats bobbed below him; tankers looked almost frozen as they flew overhead. 'Looks a bit unpleasant.' Bob gestured at the swelling sea below.

'No worries. This plane floats. Wood, you see, except for the engine and a few other bits.'

'Right, well, that's OK then.'

Joe turned towards him and grinned, white teeth gleaming. Bob was vividly reminded of Donny Osmond and would have said so except that he wasn't at all convinced that Joe was old enough to remember him.

'You can have a sleep if you want, I'll let you know when we reach the coast,' Joe said, still smiling, teeth glistening like ivory piano keys.

There was nothing else to do so Bob sat back and for the first time in weeks, even amidst the loud engine noise and whistling sounds of air streaming past, slept the sleep of the just.

Caroline lay in the dark, her body curled up in the foetal position. Her body, trying vainly to minimise the damp seeping up from the wood-strewn floor, shivered uncontrollably. She felt numb and tears fell, silently. She tried to remember and fleeting images hit her tired eyes and faded as her brain refused to function.

She could remember the hot, gut-wrenching anger as she had seen the photograph and had then run to Paul, accusations spilling over as they shouted at each other across the expanse of his flat.

He had pleaded with her then, tears welling up in his eyes as he asked her how could he have killed the old lady at the well when he had been in bed with her all night?

He would go with her to police headquarters in the morning and they would sort it out.

Wine was poured and drunk as they talked; conversation ebbed and flowed across the room as the evening light began to fade. The telephone trilled angrily at regular intervals and like her mobile phone was ignored. Suspecting the caller to be Brian, Paul swore and declared petulantly that Brian had never liked him, he was jealous and for all they knew could be setting him up to take the

MIST

blame. More angry words ricocheted off walls and furniture as Caroline tried to defend her colleagues. Finally, her throat dry from shouting, she moved shakily towards the door, her legs unsteady. He had capitulated then, taking her in his arms and holding her. There was a silence almost as loud as the previous arguments.

Much later they had walked together hand in hand across the moon soaked beach of Douglas Bay. She remembered drinking more wine, dark and heavy and tasting of blackberries, remembered going to his car and the drive along quiet country lanes, overgrown with the first lush growths of cow parsley and wild campion. He had stopped the car in a quiet country lane. Overhead trees blocked out the night sky, their boughs the living arches and pillars of some huge natural cathedral. She couldn't understand why she had left the relative safety of his car. There was a blank space where a memory ought to have been but wasn't. Fear, a small worrying voice inside her head, told her to run. He had held her closer then as if sensing her growing awareness of danger, making escape impossible.

He had walked her to a dark place of woods and then finally to a small dank, hut which leaned drunkenly against tall, ink black conifers and a rounded yellow moon. Inside he had changed; he still looked like the man she had loved but his voice became shriller, almost feminine.

'So they know, do they?'

'Know?' Caroline tried to edge towards the door but her legs wouldn't move. Her head hurt and her vision appeared to be affected. The dark interior began to swim, the floor rising up to meet her.

'Listen to me, you bitch.' His eyes glimmered black and he thrust her up against the wall, her back scraping against stone. 'By the time they find you, I'll be long gone and because they'll be searching for you, I'll be able to leave.'

'They know what you look like now, maybe I can help?' Part of her still listened to the voice of her instructor. 'Build up a rapport,' he had said, 'get the bugger on your side.' She tried to smile at him despite the growing realisation that he must have put something

MIST

in the wine. It was then that she realised who he really was. A wave of nausea hit her, hot and bilious, the rank taste stuck in her throat.

'Do they, now?' Suddenly he laughed. She hadn't realised how large and sharp his canine teeth were, like a wolf's. He pushed her legs apart and pressed himself hard up against her.

'No, please,' she whimpered. Images from other courses flooded her brain, fear triggering her urge to flee, adrenaline tiredly pumping.

'Don't worry, love, I'm not going to do anything more than I have to. And in case you're interested, I prefer it from behind if you catch my meaning. But then again, if you're offering it would be rude of me to refuse; after all, you did say please.' He leant nearer, rubbing his hands up the inside of her blouse, reaching for her breasts. Slowly he undid the front buttons and then he began to rub himself back and forth, back and forth. Caro felt sick; she couldn't move, could hardly breathe.

'Still, if it's any consolation, you won't feel much; it's the drug, you see, numbs the body, disorientates the mind, makes you much more susceptible to suggestion. Let's see now.' His voice softened to that of a whisper, almost songlike. 'Take off your clothes and then kneel down.'

To her shame, Caroline found her fingers removing cloth, pulling apart buttons and zips. Tights and pants fell in a heap on the floor. She knelt down, her skin crawling with goosebumps, an army of insects moving over her flesh. Legs buckling beneath her she felt the last of her strength ebbing into the wood strewn ground. Her hair was grabbed from behind, jerking her head back, and she prayed.

He watched her for a while, as she cowered amongst the dirt and stones and laughed, the sound ringing around the empty space. Above her he undressed, slowly dropping garments onto the ground and then he knelt beside her, a long carved blade in his hand. With his free arm he began to caress her hair, fingers moving spiderlike across her shoulders and down to massage nipples, prominent with cold.

'Do you know what the old ones did to their younger, more

MIST

attractive sacrifices?' he said, dreamily working down to her stomach and then to the curved soft round of pubic hair.

'No.' The word was squeezed out of her, her whole body trembling with the knowledge of remembered lust and loathing.

'You do know you're going to die, don't you? My little Caro, my sweet little Caro.' As he said the word 'sweet', his hand thrust inside her, kneading soft flesh and bruising skin. Caroline cried out, pain and humiliation surging through her body like a hot red mist.

Just as suddenly he stopped and stood up, kicking her with bare calloused feet.

'I'm going for a little walk. You, slut, can have a little rest and then when all is ready we will walk together to your final resting place.' He laughed then, a shrill sound. Caroline lay still, the pain inside her sharp as needles, as hard as the cold metal phallus he had held in his hand as he'd abused her. When he'd gone, still laughing, she had sunk to the floor, willing the earth to swallow her up, and prayed for death.

Later he had returned and, dragging her from the ground, he forced her into the night and away from the relative warmth of the wooden shack. Slowly she was pulled and pushed upwards along a narrow path strewn with pine needles and soft, unseen plants.

Eventually they reached the edge of the woods and began to walk, ever upwards towards a rocky knoll, dimly visible, as the light grew stronger. At the top he paused and waited. A howl rang out across the open space. Juan stood still and listened. Shrugging off the latent stirrings of unease, he pushed Caroline to the ground and waited for the first rays of the rising sun to touch the cold, grey, stones around them.

Mist rose up from the trees, slowly at first, then more quickly, blotting out the light and sounds of birds wakening. The sound of a large animal moving towards them could be clearly heard. Heather crackled and the faint swish of grasses parting echoed in the still night air. Juan swallowed and began for the first time to feel uncertain of his mission.

Juan held the heavily ornate, curved knife up towards the steadily

MIST

growing light and spoke quietly, his voice flat and empty. 'Make your peace with whoever you pray to. The time has come.'

Quickly he wrenched Caroline's head back, exposing white flesh, and held the curved blade up before bringing it down towards her neck. As the blade first bit into the soft flesh, he heard male voices calling in the mist. Figures moved within the grey smoke spreading outwards from the woods and growing ever nearer. The knife cut, a long thin red line following in the wake of cold metal. Quickly he let go his grip on the suddenly limp figure and, kneeling again, licked the wound, drinking in the iron taste of blood.

Voices called to one another, the plodding sound of large paws treading softly, growing ever closer. Juan knew the wound was a relatively shallow one. The combination of sounds and the feeling of heaviness in the knife he held had combined to ensure that the wound was not fatal. He also knew that up here amongst the heather and gorse Caroline would be dead from hypothermia within a very short space of time. Already her lips were blue tinged and the eyes, staring heavenwards, were, even now, glazed and unseeing.

Risking her being found alive, against his being caught, he ran down the slope through the thickening mist and away into the trees.

Mannanan moved quickly towards the girl and held her gently in his arms. The old trick of producing an army from leaves, sheep and mist had worked, as had holding onto the handle of the knife. The wolf could go wait for another victim; as far as he was concerned this child would live.

A grey shape crouched above the stones, lupine eyes slanted yellow and red rimmed. Saliva dripped from sharp white teeth and glinted in the growing light. Mannanan picked up a piece of flint and hurled it at the beast, cursing it in ancient Manx. The beast snarled and slunk back towards the woods.

'Caroline, Caroline,' he whispered, holding her gently in folds of white mist which, unlike the surrounding air, was warm, like steam.

She stirred. 'Please let me die,' she said, closing tired eyes, swollen with tears.

MIST

He felt the spirit within the bruised body withering, ready for its final flight, and felt a surge of anger flash within his mind.

He had always hated the waste of war and had always won with a combination of cunning, luck and outright trickery. War meant only one thing: women weeping and children starving in dirt lined ditches, too scared to run and to young to fight. They were the true casualties, not the men racing into hatred, fired up with a potent mix of mead, whiskey and hysteria, often too drunk even to know which line was friend and which foe.

Pushing thoughts of old battles away he began to sing, the song low at first, muffled but growing clearer, the sound rippling across the wet air, bubbling like a small peat brown stream. His mind merged with hers, his thoughts blotting out the memories of that night totally and utterly erasing all pain and all knowledge. Caroline sighed, her brain giving up all memory of that night from the first moment that Juan Moss revealed his true nature. Cobwebs from wakened spiders were blown across the wound, sealing it, stemming the slow flow of blood: an old soldiers' trick from wars centuries old when wise women marched alongside the men, bags of moss and herbs slung around scrawny necks and sagging breasts.

He knew that Bob Callow already had a name and a face to track down. The fact that Caroline would never remember it now was a price worth paying.

'This way you may not have a complete past but you will have a future, a chance of love and children without fear and guilt, no bitterness, no self flagellation at every turn. I hope you approve, my child, it is all I can give: that and a slim chance of life.'

He sighed and laid her gently on the ground now covered by a sheet of thick, emerald green moss, which had grown around and over stones and flints as the song he had sung had grown.

Somewhere up there above the clouds Bob would be returning. He sent thoughts spinning out, searching with his mind, and waited.

Hours later he heard the soft drone of propellers churning cold air

MIST

and drawing in his breath, blew chards of mist upwards in the pattern of a cross, its axis hovering a hundred feet above the child, still cocooned in grey steam.

Bob flew high above the Island. The little plane turned from the large verdant plains of the north towards the runway at Ronaldsway as air traffic control gave out map references and holding heights in staccato bursts of sound. As the sun-washed wings dipped, Bob saw below him a cross of white cloud.
'What the hell's that?' he asked.
'What?' asked Joe, juggling instruments and instructions.
'That cloud mass.' Bob pointed to the impossibly shaped cloud only a matter of five hundred feet below him.
'Never seen anything like that before; now, you couldn't say it was natural either, only it must be, mustn't it?'
'Can you get any closer?'
'You mean close enough to see the whites of the eyes?'
'Yes.'
'This being official?'
'Yes.'
'Only the CAA will have my hide if it isn't!'
'As official as it gets.'
'Right, hold onto your breakfast, going down.'
Joe pushed the stick down; engines whined and screamed in bad temper as they dived towards the mist-shrouded hill.
They skimmed the summit, both clearly seeing the small pale body amongst the rocks.
'Where can you land this thing?' Bob asked, fingers punching numbers on his mobile.
'Anywhere flat with a minimum of four hundred yards of grass, a width of thirty six foot and no drainage ditches.'
'Why?'
'Well, mate, the wheels dig into the ditch, the nose dips and the undercarriage gets ripped off.'
'Oh.'
'To say nothing of the owner slicing off various parts of my

MIST

anatomy with a blunt penknife and no anaesthetic. Mind, he might shoot me first, so that's all right, eh?'

Bob turned towards him, slightly shocked.

'Surely not; I mean it's police business.'

'And you really think Big Daddy Mulatto will take that into consideration?'

'Bloody Norah.'

'Exactly. We can land at Jurby. It's not too far and your lot can meet you there.'

'Will it be OK?'

'Sure. I landed there a couple of years back when I flew in the Schneider Cup race. Here we go.'

The plane began its descent, lining up above the collection of hangars and concrete buildings surrounding the old RAF base. Joe spoke quickly into his radio, giving out information and waiting impatiently for the reply.

'We can land and the helicopter's on its way. Should be here in five minutes with the paramedics. Apparently your lot had it up and flying before you rang and it's just over Maughold.'

The final turn made, Joe pressed the stick down. Flaps caught and held air, as the plane bit into the tarmac, wheels bouncing as they hit the uneven surface. Finally they stopped. Shakily, Bob emerged as a police car roared towards him, siren blaring and lights flashing. He turned and put his hand out to Joe who shook it solemnly.

'Thanks.'

'No worries and don't worry about Big Daddy, I'll sort it.'

'You sure? I could ring and . . . '

'Nah, I'll be right. Besides he's my father in law.'

Joe laughed, seeing Bob's expression, and helped Bob to remove the headset and jacket before almost pushing him out onto the wing step.

Brian Clague exited the police car almost at a run, doors slamming as he hurled himself towards Bob.

'Slow down, the chopper won't get here any quicker, even if you do have a coronary.'

'Sorry, Sir, just glad to see you.'

MIST

'So I see.'
Nothing more was said although questions hung in the air between them. Anxiously they scanned the sky and hills.
The familiar whine of the helicopter sounded overhead. It landed in a whirl of black dust, only a matter of yards away from them. A door slid open on the side and they were beckoned in. Almost immediately the insect-like machine lifted off, dust swirling in its wake. Silently Joe watched them turn into the sun and under his breath wished them luck.
It was only minutes later when they hovered above the small hill summit known as Cronk Sumark, desperately trying to find a place to land.
Bob was the first out. He looked around, hurriedly getting his bearings, and then began to run up towards the summit, coat tails flapping. As he rounded the top he saw the body being held in the arms of a dark figure. A brown hood hiding its features, the head turned towards him and eyes ancient and deep as peat pools watched him.
'Is she?' Bob asked, reaching the figures and kneeling down.
'Nearly; I've done all I can.'
Bob reached out and took the limp, almost lifeless, body from Mannanan. Caroline lay barely breathing, wrapped in fine gossamer like webs. Her body was grey and bruised, bloodstained and somehow very small.
'One thing, Bob.'
'Yes.'
'She won't remember a thing about what happened, ever.'
'Oh.'
'She wanted to die.'
'Because of what he did?'
'Yes.'
'Then it's for the best, and . . . '
'What?'
'Thank you.'
Mannanan smiled, warmth returning slowly to the dark eyes. Bob removed his coat, wrapping it around the still form. When he

MIST

turned back Mannanan had gone, as had the last strands of soft silver mist.

It was only seconds later that Brian reached the summit together with the paramedics. They bandaged, wrapped and quickly transported Caroline to the waiting machine. Brian stood rigidly watching them, fists clenched, the knuckles white.

'I'll see him in hell for this.'

Bob thrust his hands in his pocket and turned away, looking out to sea.

'You'll have to stand in line then, lad. There are a lot more in front of you and all of them with more reason than you have.'

Brian opened his mouth to speak but hurriedly closed it as he saw the expression on his superior's features.

Together they began the long climb down to the road, below where a car waited.

The noise of rotor blades gradually faded and the sheep returned to graze the higher slopes. Bob sighed wearily. He knew now that Juan had gone; somehow he could feel it. The question was, would he return? Illogically he hoped he would; there was now unfinished business. A pencil in his pocket snapped, the sound reminding him of his recent brush with the underworld. Perhaps, he thought, the lines between the law and the rest of the world were much thinner than he had previously believed.

Caroline lay in her hospital bed, tucked up in crisp white sheets, a blue blanket thrown across her feet. Brian sat by her side, holding one slim hand in his, as he had done for most of the previous day and much of the night. Several times she had woken to find him there, always on hand to administer iced water and words of comfort, tinged with the love that was growing quietly between them.

Bob found them sipping tea together, casually close, and sighing melodramatically he looked around pointedly for a chair. Brian shook his head and stood up, indicating with a nod of his head that Bob could have his.

'So,' Bob asked, patting Caroline gently on the hand. 'How are you feeling this morning?'

MIST

'Better. My head still hurts and my neck feels like it has hot pins embedded round it but otherwise I'm fine.'

'Good. I don't suppose you remember anything?'

'Not really.'

'Oh?' Bob noticed the hesitancy in the voice and leant forward. 'Anything at all, Caroline, love, anything however silly.'

Caro looked from one to the other and began nervously twisting the folds of cotton.

'I thought . . .'

'Yes.'

'Look, I can't remember anything at all about last night except for the argument in Paul, I mean Juan's flat, a walk on the beach and being driven around in the dark. But . . .'

'Go on, you're doing fine.'

'When I arrived at the flat I got the impression that Juan was preparing to leave. The thing is he couldn't have known about your visit to Manchester until I told him. Could he?'

'No, unless . . .'

'There is no way anyone from the team could have told him anything,' Brian blurted out.

'I wasn't thinking anything of the sort,' Bob replied, glaring at him. 'I may be the leader of the sorriest bunch of headless chickens this side of Watford, but I never for a moment even considered one of them of being disloyal. No, I've been wondering if our Druid was going to leave anyway.'

'Why would he do that?' asked Caroline.

'It's part of the way he seems to work; he never stays anywhere more than a year or two and he's had more than one change of name. I reckon he's left the Island for reasons of his own.'

'Will he be back?' Brian asked, covertly watching Caroline from his position propped up next to her bedside cabinet.

'I'm almost certain of that; after all he has unfinished business and come to that, so do we.'

Bob raised himself from the chair and moved towards the window. A vista of red bricks and rain flecked mortar greeted him. It matched his mood and he sighed loudly. Every bone and sinew ached with tiredness. At some point he would have to sleep and if he were lucky he'd be too tired to dream.

'Look, I'm really sorry, I just don't remember anything,' Caroline said, a catch in her voice. She had never seen her boss look so grey or so old. There were purple smudges round his eyes; he even looked as if he'd lost some of the weight he'd put on when he'd finally stopped smoking. She felt guilty and confused, her body cut and bruised but with no memory of how any of her numerous injuries had been acquired.

Bob reached out and touched her hand.

'Well, I'm not, lass. As far as I'm concerned, you can remember nothing until your dying day and I'd still be happy. Right, Brian?'

'Yes, Sir.'

'Well, I have to go see a Boss about a job; you two stay here and get some rest. Brian I shall expect you in my glory hole, first thing tomorrow morning.'

'Yes, Boss.' Brian settled back into his chair, relief showing in every muscle. He knew the bawling out would now take place in the safe confines of Bob's room and not, as he had dreaded, over the airspace above Caroline's hospital bed.

Bob stopped outside the ward and looked around for some sort of sign, hopefully with the words exit and an arrow. A trolley passed him, the contents rattling as they wafted the aroma of chicken and boiled potatoes past his nose. His nostrils twitched appreciatively. If he was going to start hankering over hospital food, he'd better eat something. Brian found him a few minutes later queuing up in the hospital canteen, plastic tray and wallet at the ready.

'Fancy seeing you in a place like this, Bob Callow!' exclaimed the lady presiding over the hot food, her face creased into a welcoming smile.

'Good grief, it can't be.'

'Oh yes it can! The pie's not bad.'

'Joan Dixon! Well, well. Pie it is then; thought you'd moved across. Didn't Don get that job in engineering, some motorway project?'

'Yes he did, and it were finished last year, so we came back. Chips?'

'Yes please, love, and some of them carrots and maybe a spoon of cabbage.'

'I'm a grandma now!'

'Never! You don't look old enough!'

'You always were a bit of a charmer; now go and pay for that lot. I've people queuing up for my services.'

'Aye, that was always the rumour.'

'Cheeky monkey!' Bob walked towards the till, grabbing a bottle of mineral water on his way. Joan watched him go, smoothed back her tightly permed, blue rinsed hair and smiled. 'Next,' she said.

He was tucking into the pie, gravy dribbling down his chin, when Brian joined him.

'Mind if I join you, Sir?' he tentatively asked, not quite sure of how far in the doghouse he was.

'Certainly, lad. And less of the Sir, it's Bob. Officially I came off duty as of five minutes ago.'

'Thanks.' Brian carefully unloaded his tray, which was almost immediately collected by a tiny wizened old woman in an apron two sizes too big. He watched as she scuttled off to collect more trays and wipe down a few tables, blue J-cloth at the ready.

'Think we could head hunt her for the canteen?' he asked, spreading butter on his jacket potato.

'My thoughts exactly,' Bob muttered, wiping gravy off his chin with a paper napkin.

'Your mum not feeding you or something?' Bob asked, pointing to Brian's over stacked plate. It wasn't so much the chicken salad but the extra large jacket potato, portion of coleslaw and a prawn cocktail which Brian was in the process of tipping onto his chicken.

'Sir? I mean Bob?'

'Never mind, lad.' They sat in a companionable silence while they ate and after he had sent Brian off for two large coffees, Bob sat back, happily replete. Upon Brian's return he leant forward and in a soft conspiratorial whisper asked the question uppermost in his mind.

'So, you and Caroline, anything I should know about?'

'We, that is, I've asked if she'd like to go for a curry and she um . . . '

MIST

'Yes?'
'She said yes.'
'I see, serious is it? Only you know the rules.'
'They may not apply.' Brian said, his voice almost a whisper.
'Oh?'
'Look, I can't say any more; she, Caroline, asked me not to . . . '
Brian stared into his mug unwilling to meet Bob's eyes, which had a definite twinkle in them.
'She's leaving the force and . . . '
'How did you . . . '
'Know. Look lad, I'm not as green as I am cabbage looking. After what that young lass has been through the only thing that surprises me is that she's in the women's surgical ward instead of psychiatric.'
'She's thinking of teaching.'
'She'd be good at that; she always enjoyed going round the schools. The kids loved her, even the older ones and you know what they can be like. I still remember our David, the moment he reached thirteen all we could get out of him were grunts or unintelligible squeals. God knows what he did at school because all he did at home was play loud house music and lie on the floor playing computer games. Oh, and he decorated his bedroom.'
'Well, that was something, then.'
'Black.'
'Black? What everything?'
'Yep. Black sheets, walls, window frame, he even painted all his furniture and the floorboards.'
'He's all right now though?'
'As far as we know, he's at Lancaster doing something in technology; ten of what I used to call 'O' levels and four 'A's to his credit. Oh, and Mark, who wouldn't say boo to the proverbial goose and had the sex appeal and charisma of a wet lettuce, got into Edinburgh to study engineering, joined a student jazz band and is apparently knee deep in young nubile women. Or so the wife tells me. I don't know; after all I'm only their Dad.'
'So they're doing all right?'

MIST

'Seems so,' Bob said, parental pride writ large over his satisfied features.

'Bob?'

'Yes lad?'

'Will she ever remember anything?'

'Who, our Caroline?'

'Yes.'

'Not as far as the medical profession can tell. Mind you, getting any sort of firm opinion from any of them is like striking gold in Laxey. You know, I reckon half of them wouldn't give you their names unless they had to.'

'Oh.'

'Caroline will be fine; just give her a day or two for the wounds to start healing and she'll be bossing us about like she always used to.'

'One of the doctors said something about cobwebs. That her neck was wrapped in them. He thought that if they hadn't been there to stem the bleeding she would have died. The thing is, I can't see why Juan Moss would cut her throat and then try to bandage it. I mean cobwebs?'

'Nothing wrong with that; the ancient Celts used webbing like we would use gauze to encourage the blood to clot and to stem the flow of bleeding. And before you ask I am one hundred per cent sure of the fact that Juan Moss did not have second thoughts, if that's what worries you.'

'But?'

'No buts, trust me: I know. And before you ask, no, I'm not going to tell you any more; after all that's the sort of thing which keeps you a detective constable and me detective inspector. Right?'

'Right.' Brian smiled, relief evident in his eyes.

'Anything else you want to ask, while I'm at my most sociable?'

'Just one thing, it's been bothering me, apart from the spider webs. How did Caroline survive the cold? She was naked for hours, she should have died from hypothermia.'

'And this is a complaint, is it?'

'No, I'd just . . . ' Brian's voice tailed off.

'Look lad.' Bob leant forward until their heads almost touched, his voice a soft whisper. 'There are more things in heaven and earth. Need I say more? Caroline is alive, a miracle if you like or a fluke if you don't believe in miracles. Thing is, I believe in more than just us, the likes of you and me. If, say, some guardian angel or spirit was watching over young Caroline with orders possibly from the big boss upstairs and because of that she survived the Mad Druid, I'm not going to be making any complaints and nor should you. Our job is to search and find this madman and when we do, to do our best to ensure that he's brought to trial and then locked away for a very long time.'

'Right.'

'It is not our job to spend precious time speculating on the impossible; leave that to the theologians. Understood?'

'Loud and clear. Do you want me to help search the woods for clues?'

'No, you stay here, look after Caroline, help her fill in a few application forms or arrange a holiday together, only don't let her brood.'

'Yes, Bob.' Brian stood up and in the act of walking back to the ward, stopped and turned back to Bob who had remained seated. 'Thanks,' he said and then as if he sensed that maybe he had said too much, scurried off towards the exit.

It was several hours later, whilst searching the woods below Cronk Sumark, that they found the hut where Juan Moss had taken his most recent victims. But when found, it took only seconds for Bob to realise that it was the place he had been searching for for so long.

Forensic were like children on the beach, turning over logs and stones, bagging everything they could remove. Slowly the haul of items became larger, including a white stick and what looked like a long length of silver chain.

Outside, prodding damp earth and tree roots with a length of bamboo, a young Police Constable discovered the unmistakable sheen of a black plastic bag, the sort used for garden refuse. The stench was unmistakable. Timidly he poked it; it felt soft. Feeling suddenly unsure and very nauseous he called for back-up, hurriedly standing to one side as one of the forensic team felt the outer layer of shiny plastic with thick rubber gloves. He looked up frowning as Bob made his way over.

'Feels like a skull of some kind, not human: too small and the wrong shape, dog perhaps or cat. Won't know till we cut it open.'

'Better do it back at the lab; my bet is it's the skull of a small terrier and matches the dog's body we found at Mrs Skilliton's.'

Bob almost backed into a tree as the bag was carried gingerly past him to a waiting van and a large plastic airproof box.

Almost simultaneously a cry rang out from the interior of the hut and Geoff emerged bearing something round and brown in colour. As Bob moved closer, he could see the gaping eye sockets and realised it was a skull, a human skull.

Bob swallowed. 'Ah,' he said, trying not to show the revulsion he felt.

'Not recent, and we can't find any more of the skeleton, just this,' Geoff replied, carefully turning it in the bright sunshine.

'Any sign of damage?'

'Large crack across the back and the jaw has been smashed at some point; oh yes, and we found a scrap of paper inside the eye socket. Looks like a till receipt with brownish writing; could be blood, won't be able to tell until the lab gets going.'

'Is it legible?'

Bob gingerly took the proffered plastic bag containing a small slip of paper and peered at it.

'Partially, needs cleaning up a bit first but roughly speaking it just has a date and a place,' Geoff replied, taking the bag back.

'Mind passing that piece of information on, before the lab verifies it?' Bob asked impatiently.

'Well, it looked like five dash seven, and underneath Mans fort.'

'Right, well, off you go and find out for sure and let me know how old it is. I have a feeling it may be our first victim's late husband.'

Bob rubbed his hands together and looked up towards the blue sky peering between the tall heads of conifers. There was nothing

MIST

much more he could usefully do and so he started to walk back to his car, already rehearsing in his head what exactly he would say at the fast approaching meeting with the Chief Constable and the Minister in charge of law and order.

Tavistock had eventually arrived in Newcastle and had taken a taxi to her hotel. The hotel was new and modern, overlooking the entrance to the Tyne and the long stretch of coast which curved back on itself at the river's mouth. Ships, which towered above the low red brick building, slid past her bedroom window, the sound deadened by the almost new double glazing.

Slowly she unpacked, trying to shrug off the tiredness that threatened to close her eyes as she walked around the room. In desperation she brushed her teeth and washed her face with cold water. 'Perhaps,' she thought 'all I need is to feel a bit cleaner.' Nothing happened; she still felt as if she could sleep for a week. She was debating in her head as to whether she ought to just ring her friend Roger and explain that she was going to be a bit late, when the phone rang. It was Roger.

'I'm in reception, the car's parked right outside and the kids are gagging to impress you with their talent and dedication. Actually they're more than likely behind the warehouse having a quiet fag and trying to remember their lines but don't tell 'em I said so.' Roger paused, listening to the silence on the other end of the line. 'You all right?' he asked, suddenly concerned.

'Yes, fine, just a bit tired, long day yesterday,' Tavistock replied.

'Well then, what you need is a good walk in some bracing North Sea air. I will personally escort you for a walk round this fine edifice of architectural simplicity and then we'll shoot off, how's that sound?' Tavistock smiled despite herself. In the background she could hear the young girl on reception laughing.

'Give me a minute to put on some shoes and grab my coat and I'll be down,' she said.

'Right you are, then. I'll wait here and extract some interesting life stories from this very attractive young lady.' Tavistock could hear more laughter as the phone was disconnected, and smiled.

MIST

Roger would only need a minute or so to acquire yet another idea that he would eventually weave into the story line of one of the next scripts he was working on. Tavistock had met Roger originally at the BBC when she had been engaged on recording an interview for Radio 4 Manchester. Roger was writing and producing a script for some award winning series about North Sea fishermen and they had met over coffee and runny shepherd's pie in the BBC canteen. They had talked, recognised a mutual interest in promoting youth orientated drama and script production, and had since whenever possible helped to promote the other's pet project of the moment. Roger was currently working on a film setting out the problems the young had with peer pressure, sex and drugs. The film was aimed at spreading awareness among fourteen- and fifteen-year-olds and would hopefully be included in a series of short films which were being collected by the BBC's educational department. His previous film, based around a struggling football club, was being premiered that evening at the Customs House and Tavistock had been invited to help. Her job was to encourage the press to turn up and to persuade another old friend, Angela Benning, now head buyer for Channel Four films, to come up from London to watch it.

She collected her coat from the chair over which she had thrown it and stepped into her shoes.

A few minutes later she found herself being frogmarched around the outside of the hotel. Salt laden spray sandblasted her cheeks and tried to rip her coat off. Later, satisfied by the change in his companion's condition – Tavistock had stopped yawning after the first blast of cold air had bruised her tonsils – Roger allowed Tavistock to take temporary refuge in his car.

They arrived some time later at the old warehouse, where current filming was taking place. A group of youngsters stood in the doorway apparently at loggerheads over something, and Roger, taking one look, applied the brakes, cut the engine and exited with dark mutterings to find the Director. Tavistock watched as the youngsters parted for him like the Red Sea and Roger, not unlike Moses on a bad day, strode off into the gloomy interior.

After waiting for a minute or two, Tavistock left the warm snug confines of the car and, curious to see how the film was progressing, quietly entered the warehouse entranceway.

Tavistock walked cautiously around the lower floor, her eyes gradually becoming accustomed to the dark, dust-laden light. The camera crew hired from Mersey television stood around checking equipment and moving heavy lengths of black plastic coated wire. A young man sporting a long blond ponytail was taking light readings and sighing in a highly theatrical manner. Some of the cast were rehearsing amidst an assortment of old oil drums and pallet boards, their voices carrying eerily towards her. Her foot kicked absentmindedly at the floor. Dust and dirt moved aside to reveal a small silver coloured disc. It glittered in a sudden shaft of light as one of the high intensity film lights was switched on. Quickly she stooped and picked it up. It appeared to be a medallion with a crude picture of St. Christopher carrying a child across an expanse of tossing waves.

Something, a noise, a glimmer of movement, made her look up towards the rusting girders above her head. A shape was clambering above her, a dark shadow moving slowly along the main beam, shuffling and trembling, its breathing that of a geriatric with emphysema.

'Stand up, you little shite!' a figure beside her shouted. 'Stand up and walk.'

The figure rose slowly, trembling and began to inch its way along the beam. Tavistock watched in fascinated horror. Beside her other figures now stood looking upwards. One of them was crying silently, tears coursing down her face. Tavistock turned her gaze away from the youth above and watched the girl. She was very young, her body as yet not fully defined. The clothes she wore were cheap looking and dirty. A sleeve was torn and several of the front buttons were missing. The young man beside her, the one who had shouted, was holding her arm. He turned to her and whispered something Tavistock couldn't catch. The girl recoiled, pushing him away; others crowded round, silently goading him on.

The girl screamed as she was pushed to the ground; hands helped to hold her down. Tavistock could almost taste the fear in the air.

MIST

The leader of the gang pushed something into the girl's mouth and then poured a clear looking liquid from a bottle down her throat. There was a sharp cry from above. They all looked up as the figure screamed obscenities at them.

The girl, now still, began to moan quietly. The leader knelt down looking up towards the figure standing motionless above.

'Watch and learn,' he said and then he began slowly to unzip his jeans.

'No!' The scream reached them almost as the body, losing its balance, fell to the floor. Blood billowed out behind the skull, fragments of bone and skin littering the concrete floor. His hands clenched, body twitching convulsively as the final nerve spasms lifted dead limbs for a final brief moment. Beside him the rape continued. The girl lay silent, eyes glazed as liquid oozed from her mouth.

'Pigeons?'

'What!' Startled, Tavistock turned to find Roger standing behind her.

'Pigeons, up there. They play hell with the camera lenses, always leaving little messages from a great height.' Roger watched her, suddenly concerned. 'What's up? You look like you've seen a ghost.'

Tavistock looked around again, focussing on the present day. The crew moved around setting up microphones and extra lights. The actors and actresses stood or sat around as the final touching up of their makeup was applied with large brushes and small tubs of pale powder. Clearly startled, she flinched as the lights around the central area were switched on. The film she had thought she was seeing had never happened, or had it?

'Roger, tell me, did anything happen here, maybe twenty odd years ago?'

'Why?'

'Was there?'

'Maybe.'

'Roger!'

'Look, there was something a long time ago, a friend told me about it. You know that book I was writing in the eighties, about

MIST

that youth gang that went out of control, well, he was helping me and I interviewed this woman. Actually her kid is one of the extras in the film you'll be seeing tonight.'

'Can I speak to her?'

'I'll introduce you to her tonight. She may not talk to you, mind. She didn't say much the last time and I'd poured enough vodka into her to collapse a Russian. Only first you get out of here, walk along and say hello to the North Sea. I'm not taking you anywhere with a complexion even a shade would add makeup to.'

'Fine, I'll go back to the hotel then; see you tonight?'

'Seven thirty at the side entrance, round the back; remember, same place we met up before that play *The Night Watch*.'

Tavistock took a final look around and turned, walking back to the sun-drenched world outside. Roger stood still, watching her retreating back. He shivered and then moved on towards his team of young thespians. He hated this particular location; it always made him think of graveyards and ghosts.

Later that evening Tavistock stood chatting with various VIPs and members of the cast after the first official screening of the new film. Voices ebbed and flowed around her as the project was toasted with copious quantities of rather palatable Argentinean wine. Out of the corner of one eye she was aware of Roger working the room, making introductions and smoothing down any potential ruffled feathers. The lady beside her was still talking about her son's writing career and she bent her head forward to listen and at least gather enough information sensibly to answer the lady's next question.

'Ah, there you are. I'd like you to meet a friend of mine.' Roger stood behind her, a companion at his side. Tavistock smiled at the lady still talking about some residency in the States, and said, 'I really hate to stop you in mid flow but I'd like to introduce you to Roger Hanson, the producer of the film we've just watched.'

The woman pinked with pleasure and fluttered dark blue eyelashes at him.

'You must be so proud, Mr Hanson. I thought it was lovely. Some

MIST

of the language was a bit, well, you know... Anyway, it was very good. You know, my son, he's in the States you know and he wants to write for films and I was wondering...' Still talking, she walked off her arm interlinked with Roger's. Tavistock watched them go. The public could be very fickle, she thought, especially hers.

'Well, she could have at least said goodbye!' announced her new companion. Tavistock turned and found herself face to face with the girl she had seen in the warehouse that morning. The woman looked calmly back at her. Her eyes were dark and intelligent, the body slightly wider than before and her hair, which was now short and permed, clung to an over made-up face in soft copper coloured wisps.

'Are you really Tavistock Allan, the writer?' she said, reaching out for another glass of wine as one of the cast passed them by, precariously balancing a tray of glasses with unsteady hands. The girl carrying the tray looked up and, seeing who it was, grinned; her face softened and looked years younger.

'Mum!'

'Thanks, love, you couldn't take the empty back too; I don't know what to do with it.'

'OK.'

'The film was good, especially your bit. I was dead proud.' She beamed at her daughter and hugged her. The glasses on the tray rattled threateningly, wine slopped onto the metal surface and dripped off the edge.

'Mum!' The girl took a step back, nearly colliding with a tall man carrying a plate of sandwiches and vol-au-vents. 'Look I have to go, I'll see you tomorrow, yeah?'

Without waiting the girl moved away towards a crush of young people almost glued to the back wall.

'My daughter.'

'She's very talented; wasn't she the one that escorted the old lady to hospital and then fell in love with the grandson?' Tavistock asked.

'Yes, and she had that singing bit at the end. This...' The woman turned and gestured, covering the whole room with red-taloned hands, 'is the beginning for my Mel. The way out.'

MIST

'You two behaving yourselves?' Roger asked from behind them. They moved further apart so he could join the conversation. 'Sorry I couldn't stay to do the introductions, but I'm back now. Tavistock, this is Sandra Taylor. Sandra, Tavistock Allan the writer.'

'Ooh,' Sandra cooed, very obviously pleased with her new companion. 'I love your books, always take one on holiday. I really liked that one about the homicidal sheep farmer. Tell me...' she leant forward in a conspiratorial manner, 'do they really do that sort of thing, you know with the wellingtons, like in your book?'

Tavistock blushed and Roger, who hadn't read her latest tome, made a mental note to borrow his wife Pam's copy as soon as he got home.

'No, well, maybe; look, it was just something I heard in a pub in Cornwall and I put it in.'

'Oh, so you didn't actually research that bit then?'

Tavistock, who had just taken a large mouthful of red wine, nearly choked at the mental image of Richard arriving home to find a sheep, a pair of green Wellingtons and several large men, busily engaged in his wife's research.

'No, we, um, sometimes leave it to the experts and just write it up.'

'Sometimes we watch videos.' Roger piped up. Tavistock tried to tread on his feet and failing to make contact, desperately gave him her best 'drop dead' look. Roger, taking no notice whatsoever, continued blithely on: 'Now, Sandra, Tavistock is writing a new book on youth cultures and I was wondering if you could tell her the story about the one your brother was involved in.'

'Neville?'

'Yes.'

'Why?' Her face drained of colour, almost as if someone had turned on a tap. She looked nervously round.

'You don't have to, I mean Roger just said he thought you had a story I might find interesting but it's not essential. Tell me what do you do.'

Sandra brightened and the colour slowly ebbed back.

MIST

'I'm a machinist, for a knicker factory. Not bad money really, considering.'

Roger shook his head at them and sighed before moving on to the group of smartly suited members of the borough council, busily engaged in chatting up his amply proportioned camera woman.

Sandra watched him go, a faint frown passing across her face. 'Look, I can tell you a bit of what you want but not here. Too many people I know.'

'Great, how about over sandwiches and champagne at my hotel; we can order room service and you won't be overheard. Besides which my feet are killing me and I would dearly love to take these smart but horribly tortuous shoes off!' Tavistock smiled at Sandra: a real smile, not the public one she habitually had to wear. Sandra, after a moment's thought, smiled back.

'Why not?' she replied.

Carefully they manoeuvred their way towards the exit. A taxi in the act of dropping a fare off in the surrounding car park was hastily commandeered and given instructions.

Sandra sat back and visibly relaxed. 'That was dead lucky, we could have been hanging around for hours out there.'

Tavistock, watching her, felt intuitively that here was someone who knew something very important. The question was, would she actually let the information go?

When they arrived at the hotel, dinner was still being served and Tavistock, who really felt in need of something more substantial than sandwiches, broached the question of whether Sandra would prefer a meal instead? Sandra looked around her and nodded, never one to let an opportunity go and rightly thinking that she would meet no one she really knew, Sandra marched into the restaurant as if to the manor born. The waitress, on seeing them enter, scurried forward, anxious to have their order as soon as possible. The quicker they ordered the quicker it could be prepared and the quicker she could go home.

'Imagine me having dinner with someone famous!' Sandra looked around, evidently pleased. 'Look, I've got a camera in my handbag;

137

MIST

do you reckon the waitress would take a photo of the two of us?' she whispered, extracting the camera as she spoke.

'I would have thought so,' Tavistock replied. 'Ah, here she comes; what do you want?' Sandra picked up the menu in front of her and after several minutes of mouth watering thought, made her final decision. The waitress stood beside their table, pen poised and lips pursed. When they had finished ordering and the photograph had been taken, Sandra and Tavistock sat back and mutually regarded the other.

The wine waitress returned a few minutes later, bearing an opened bottle of champagne.

'Oooh, you know, they are never going to believe this at home.'

'Call me Tavistock, Sandra. After all, at the moment you're helping me with my research; normally I'd have to pay a fee or something so this is a sort of thank you.'

'Oh well, in that case.' Sandra took a long sip and then, placing the glass back almost reverently, sighed with satisfaction, finally beginning to relax.

'We had some of the fizzy stuff at our Colin's do, but it was one of them sparkling wines; it might be made the same way and very nice but you can't beat the real thing, can you.'

'No, no, you can't. So have you lived here a long time?'

'Yes, I was born here. I did go away once on one of them government training things but I soon came back.'

The starter arrived as they began to find out more about each other, the conversation widening to include family and friends as they ate. The rest of the meal passed pleasantly enough and finally, over coffee, Tavistock carefully broached the subject around which they had both, in their own way, circled all evening. The restaurant was clearing up as they left to meander down the hallway. The simplest thing seemed to be to sit in Tavistock's suite and finish off the second bottle of champagne. They took the lift to the first floor and finally sank into separate easy chairs. The bottle and glasses sat on the coffee table between them.

'This is nice,' Sandra said, looking round and easing swollen feet from three inch high heeled shoes.

MIST

'Yes, it's not bad. You should have seen some of the places I stayed in, when I first started writing. Some were so small you had to climb over the bed to get to the bathroom. Bathroom! The kids have bigger toy boxes!' replied Tavistock as she stood up to discard shoes now at least one size smaller than when she had first put them on, that morning.

'So,' said Sandra relaxing against the soft back of the chair. 'Why did you want to talk to me. I mean the real reason?'

Tavistock, in the act of settling herself back into her chair, stopped.

'How do you mean?' she asked, suddenly wary.

'I think you know.' Sandra sat quite still, her eyes closed, arms folded in front of her.

Tavistock moved to the window and stared out at the dark star-studded sky. The moon gleamed, light reflected in the water. Slowly a cloud edged across its face, blotting out the hard white rays. Below, the lunar reflection quivered and was suddenly gone.

'I thought I saw something today, but I couldn't have. It was after I found this.'

Carefully she extracted the silver medallion from her jacket pocket and without looking at Sandra's face placed it on the table in front of her.

Sandra bent wordlessly towards the object and, seeing what it was, pushed the table away and stood up to face Tavistock. Her eyes blazed and her whole body trembled, hands clenched in fists at her side.

'Where did you get it? Did Roger tell you? Is this the way you spice up your books; the gutter press could learn a lot from you.' Sandra paused, her breath coming in shallow gasps. 'And what do you mean you saw something, saw what?' Hysterically she paced the room, picking up her discarded belongings of bag, shoes and coat.

'If I tell you what I know, will you promise not to say anything to anyone,' Tavistock pleaded, her voice harsh.

Sandra stopped in the act of pushing her feet back into her shoes and looked at Tavistock. What she saw in her face seemed to reassure her and she returned to her chair and sat back down.

MIST

'All right, I'll listen, but I warn you this had better be special.'

'Oh it is, it is.' Tavistock answered.

'Right well, off you go then,' Sandra said, picking up a wine glass and pouring herself a generous helping.

Tavistock sat on the edge of the windowsill and talked. She related how she, or rather her son, had found the first body, how she had discovered her gift for seeing back into the past and finally she told Sandra what she had seen that day in the old abandoned warehouse. There was silence afterwards; the wind moaned beyond the windows, clouds moving in a heaped bunch of black towards the land over the sea. It was when Tavistock finally looked up from the carpet she had been staring at while she told her tale, that she realised Sandra was softly crying, tears coursing down her face, black runnels of mascara marring her cheeks. Tavistock picked up a box of tissues from the elongated dressing table and passed them silently to Sandra. Sandra took one, muttering her thanks. Finally she looked up, meeting Tavistock's anxious eyes.

'I'm sorry,' she said, wiping away more tears.

'No need, you have every right to be upset. Have you ever talked about this to anyone?' Tavistock asked.

'No, not really; people talked to me, told me to buck up and get on with my life. You know what one stupid cow said? She said in this posh university voice, "You'll be fine, pretty girl like you, you'll have them queuing up." You know what, I haven't had a man since, they touch me and I run screaming for the door. Almost broke some poor bastard's arm once and all because he tried to kiss me goodnight, and I'd known him years too.'

'I really don't know what to say.' Tavistock said, meaning it.

'Nothing to say.' Sandra took another gulp of wine and leant over the table to pour out some more. 'Perhaps I should have told someone, I mean told them everything, got it clear in my mind. Bet some shrink would have had a field day, eh?' She laughed, the sound forced, the laughter hollow, a nasty edge to it.

'You know what, I will tell you. I'll start at the beginning and end at the end. You can even tape it if you like; after all, that's what you writers do, isn't it?'

'Well yes, if you're sure, otherwise I'll just listen.'

'No, you tape it. It might be of some use; you can let that copper, the one you was at school with, listen; he might learn something about the bastard he's after, eh?'

Tavistock bent down and rummaged in her bag to find her small tape machine. She inserted a new tape, dropping the cellophane wrapper onto the floor. The machine was placed on the table next to the bottle and before going any further she poured out two more glasses and handed one to Sandra. Sandra took it, sipped the top and, eyes closed, began to talk.

'The gang started as an offshoot of an older one. The parent gang, if you want to call it that, started off as a sort of tenants' association protection racket, only they went too far in the end. Our gang started because one of the youths involved with it decided he needed a gang to protect him from the original gang and started recruiting. As far as I could see, all the recruits had one thing in common.'

'They were all hard cases?'

'No, that was the odd part, they weren't. In fact it was the opposite if anything; we were all victims of some kind. Trev, that was the name of the kid in charge, was sort of charismatic. When my daughter Mel did modern history at school, she had to watch these old ciné films of Hitler. She brought one home of him addressing the youth movement and he reminded me of Trev. They had the same eyes and they both had this way of talking so that you believed every word, even though it made no sense afterwards. Trev told us we had to be strong, we had to contact our spiritual side, the earth in all of us. He called it wakening the beast, or wolf, or something. Like I said, it seemed to make perfect sense at the time. Neville, my brother, joined first. He was always getting picked on at school. He, well, he wasn't quite right; he had these mood swings, he'd get violent and then he'd stop and run away crying. He was really bright but he couldn't read words properly or understand the questions when they were written down but he'd copy you if you made something and showed him how. And then there was the counting.'

'Counting?'

MIST

'Yes, he wouldn't go up the stairs at night unless he tapped the end of the banister seven times; he wouldn't even go up a flight of steps unless you could divide the number of steps by three. He used to have this thing about washing as well. Don't get me wrong, he was the best brother anyone could have. He was just a bit odd, weird really. Anyway, the bottom line was that the other older boys at school sensed it and they used to pick on him a lot. Trev befriended him. He was, I think, in the top year and lived at some children's home. Trev sort of took him under his wing; he was probably the only one there, apart from the teachers, that gave a toss.' Sandra sighed.

'Go on, so Neville joined, did he?'

'Yes, there was what Trev called an "initiation ceremony" in one of the disused railway sheds down at the freight depot. Nev went there one night after school and he didn't get back until the next day. Our Da went mad, beat him with his belt. You know, Nev never cried once but at the end he turned on Da and said in this really weird voice that if he ever did anything like that again he'd kill him. I remember our Neville's face even now; it was dead like he didn't even care. Frankly, I couldn't give a toss what happened to Da; after all, he wasn't our real dad. Come to think of it, he wasn't the first and our Gran always said me and Nev had different dads anyway. Not when Mum was around though, she'd have gone spare.'

'What happened then?'

'Nothing much. Nev continued to go round with this gang and a bloke called Joe asked me out. I was thirteen at the time and well, you know, at that age if you don't have a boyfriend your mates think you're a les, so I went out with him. To be honest, I didn't really spend much time worrying about Nev because of going out with Joe and we'd started doing all this work towards exams and such. Then something happened at school and to protect me Nev asked me if I'd like to join the gang.'

'Why? What happened?'

'There was this kid called Gloria Evans, biggest tits in the school and the biggest mouth. She used to pick on the new girls, get them

MIST

to steal fags, booze and stuff and then she started picking on me. One night she caught me coming back from the chippie, pushed me to the ground and peed on the chips. I was so scared I ran all the way home. Told Da I'd tripped and the chips was ruined. He beat me almost senseless till Ma put a stop to it.'

'How did she do that?'

'Grabbed the belt so he turned on her. In the row that followed I slunk upstairs and found Nev. After that I went to the next meeting. Perhaps it would have been better if I'd just run away like I was going to.'

'Are you OK, we can stop if you like?'

'No, I, I haven't thought about this for years. I think maybe I should have said something before; it's just that it was easier to forget.' Sandra drained her glass, her hands unsteady. Outside the wind had reached storm force and was howling and moaning against the outer walls of the hotel. Spray lashed at the wide picture windows and clouds purple against the black sky raced each other against a clear green tinged moon. Sandra watched the battle waging between sea and wind. After a few minutes she started again, her voice low and strained.

'We met the others at an old abandoned warehouse, down on the docks. I couldn't see anyone's face clearly but I recognised the voices. One was Gloria's.'

'The bully?'

'The very same. I thought, this is it, I'm dead meat, only she was really nice, said how good it was to see me and the really scary part was that she seemed to mean it. She even put her arm round my shoulder and she trembled. I can still remember the scared look in her eye and then I turned round and there was this figure standing against the door, sort of framed by the light outside, just like in them spaghetti westerns. He walked towards us and I saw that it was Trev. He was carrying this big black box.

'He never said nothing, just took out some chalk, drew a circle and then surrounded it with candles stuck in old beer bottles. When he'd lit them he told everyone to sit around the light and he gave everyone a plastic cup. I don't know what he poured into it, some

MIST

sort of alcohol, it could have been cheap vodka. Ma kept some in a cupboard under the sink and when I was about nine or ten Nev and I pinched it, to see what it tasted like. It were bloody awful and I had this headache for days after. The stuff he gave us tasted sort of sweet and bitter at the same time. It must have had something in it because after a while I felt numb but I could hear and see all right, just couldn't move. And then we waited in this cold silence. Even the birds in the roof had stopped calling to each other. I remember watching the flames flickering and then Trev stood up and started to walk round us. He kept saying, "Who has the Power?" And everyone answered, "You do." This went on for some time, Then he went on about wolves and things, like I said before. Finally he called for the new members to stand up. Two of us did. I was one and Joe was the other. You know, I hadn't realised he was there till then.'

'You could move; had the drink, drug, whatever, worn off?'

'No, I don't think so, but somehow we could move only if he, Trev, told us to.'

'Oh, I see.'

'You do?'

'Yes, I'm afraid I do. I'll tell you why later.'

'He went round to Joe first and told him to walk the walk of the damned, as every initiate had to. I could see Joe hesitating. He looked at me and then he walked to a ladder at the side of the wall and began to climb up. I remember Trev shouting at him to stand up and then it all becomes a blur. Nev took me home. He didn't say anything to me at all. My clothes were all torn and there was blood on my skirt and down my legs. I could hardly walk and Nev kept picking me up and then he'd sit on the pavement and cry that it was all his fault.

'Ma had waited up for us; the old man was out. I remember she put me in the bath and burnt my clothes. Then she put me to bed. Nev and she talked for hours. At any moment I expected Da to come home and belt me one for ruining my things but he never did. The police came round the next morning and spoke to Ma. After that a doctor came and a priest. The weirdest thing was that no-one spoke to me, they spoke round me. Ma went to Mass every morning and night and Da still didn't come home. About a week later I went to get something from under the sink and I saw a wrapper from the fish supper we'd had the night before; it must have fallen behind the bin. There was a photograph of Da on the front. I took it up to my room and read it.'

'What did it say?'

'Da had been found floating in the docks. He'd been stabbed over thirty times with what they thought was an army knife. Joe had also been found on a piling, all tangled up with bits of old net and wood. The police said that Joe had raped me, when high on drugs and drink, that as I was under-age my Da had gone mad, gone after him and had been stabbed to death. The prints on the knife that killed him were Joe's and afterwards they reckoned he'd slipped on the blood while throwing my old man in the docks, fallen in and cracked his skull open on the concrete pilings. I was so angry that no one had told me, I waited for Nev to get home and told him I was going to the police and I was going to tell them that Joe never raped me, or killed Da, because he was dead. Nev turned on me then, said that if I did they'd find out that killing Da was part of the bargain he'd made with Trev for allowing me to have the protection of the gang. That Joe had fallen from the girders accidentally and that if we said anything Ma would be next. So that was that.'

'Did you ever go back?'

'No. Shortly afterwards I found out I was pregnant, and the world changed completely. School was out so I was taught at home and one of them refuges for unmarried mothers. I didn't want the baby but Ma was Catholic so there was no choice, even with the amount of men she'd had. I tried starving myself, gin in the bath, knitting needle, the lot. Nine months later I gave birth to a little girl and I hated her. The night she was born she stopped breathing and died while I watched. There was a girl in the next bed who cried all the time. She was going to University until some lad got her pregnant. She kept saying she'd end up like her Ma, forty going on seventy five with eight kids and a council slum. So I swapped the baby.'

'What!'

'She didn't want hers any more than I wanted mine, but for

MIST

different reasons. I knew the baby was Trev's. He came round to see me and said that as long as I was the mother of his child I was safe. Maybe he knew what I'd been trying to do or maybe he fancied the evil carrying on after he'd gone or some crap like that. I didn't mind having a baby, it was an excuse not to go back to school and the council had promised us a new flat – better area, nearer the shops and everything. So I swapped the babies. No one knew; it was the dead of night. I gave the dead child to the kid in the next bed and fed her child. Swapped the tags, clothes, everything. The kid never knew what I'd done and even if she did she never said nothing.

'About four in the morning the nurse came in to check that everything was all right. All the curtains went round this poor kid's bed and the poor cow cried for hours. I still remember the look she gave me when I pulled the curtain aside to see how she was. It was the look of relief, the sort a man condemned to die would give if they'd been pardoned. After that my conscience was clear. Ma came to collect me about ten days later, I'd picked up some infection the day after the baby was born and been really ill. Ma said that at one point they all thought I was going to die. When I got home my Gran was there. Nev had committed suicide; he left a note explaining that it was all his fault and he couldn't live with himself. He never said why, just tied a noose round his head and jumped from the girder in the old warehouse. Kids playing found him days later.'

'And the gang?'

'Disbanded. The police cracked down on everyone. Trev disappeared; I heard he'd moved south. Everybody else moved or died. I brought up my child as well as I could and that was that, until I started reading about those murders in the Isle of Man. That's what this is really all about, isn't it?'

'Yes, how did you know?'

'I'll tell you over a coffee. I feel like I'm nearly sober.'

'Right.' Tavistock moved to the kettle and hospitality basket and made two coffees. She returned slowly, carefully placing the coffee on the table with creamers, sugar and some biscuits.

'We get a card from Trev every year on my Mel's birthday. The last one was from Douglas, Isle of Man. So when I heard about the Mad Druid and how the police suspected drugs had been used, I wondered.'

'Why didn't you say something?'

'Oh come on, who'd believe me? Besides which, I thought that it would all come out, maybe the girl in the next bed would remember me, and if they wanted to do one of them DNA tests on Mel they'd find out about everything. I love my little girl, you see, always have, she's the only thing that's stood between me and the loony bin at times. Besides, it was a long time ago and he, Trev that is, could be perfectly respectable.'

'Only you don't think so?'

'No, no, I don't.'

The room was silent as they drank their coffee, the first rays of light piercing the gloom outside.

'I'll have to tell the police what you suspect.'

'But not about Mel?'

'No, not about that. Did she die in her sleep, Trev's child?'

'Sort of. I kinda helped, with a pillow.'

'I think maybe in your position I would have done the same.'

'What about the tape?'

'We can wipe that bit, now, between us.'

Together they listened to their voices, editing the relevant chatter. Satisfied, Sandra sat back, staring at the lights twinkling on the water outside.

'There was one other thing. The paper said they still hadn't traced the drug. This might be nothing but when they found Joe he had a small piece of a white tablet, tucked in some plastic. It was still clenched in his fist. It was a funny name, sounded like Diplodocus. I remember because Joe's little brother was dino mad and he went on about them all the time. I'll write down the names and dates if you like.'

Tavistock silently handed over a piece of paper and pencil and Sandra wrote down the information, her tongue poking between gleaming white teeth, her face rapt with concentration. Tavistock tried to imagine how she would have felt in her position, abused,

MIST

raped and at the centre of an ongoing police investigation, all before her fourteenth birthday. A year celebrated by the arrival of a child, the unloved result of being raped by what to any girl would have seemed like the Devil himself. She moved to the window and looked out as the sun began to rise. She turned back to find Sandra sleeping gently, her mouth open and uncaring, her face lit by the first gold rays. Tavistock gently tucked a blanket from the spare bed round her and made herself another coffee, which she drank whilst she watched the storm abating with the falling of the tide and the return of daylight.

Tavistock rang Bob from the hotel, as soon as Sandra had left together with another bottle of champagne. They had parted almost tearfully; promises of books being forwarded and the occasional postcard were made. It took some time to get through to Bob which made Tavistock very wary: had something else happened in her absence?

'Yes?' barked a well known voice.

'Bob.'

'Ah, Tavistock.'

'Has something happened?'

'You mean apart from the attempted rape and murder of Caroline, my recently assigned detective constable, who incidentally is in hospital? And last but not least the fact that we know who Juan Moss is?'

'Some guy called Trev?'

'That's right, Trevor Mulatto; how did you know?'

'Stayed up last night with a lady who knew him, shall we say, intimately but only as Trev.'

'Ah, you mean an old flame? Although frankly, after what happened to Caroline I sincerely doubt that he'd know love if it got up and bit him on the...!'

'Bob!'

'All right, all right, I'll keep it clean. Do I gather, from your icy tone of voice, that this woman would not welcome him with open arms?'

MIST

'Bob let's just put it this way: he raped her at thirteen, murdered her boyfriend, had her father knifed to death Julius Caesar style and was instrumental in the suicide of her brother.'
'Good God! Anybody else.'
'Don't know but she did say that most of the people in this particular gang that Trev ran were either dead or had disappeared.'
'Ah, he's been a busy boy, then.'
'So if you know who he is, do you have him?'
'Not exactly, he's sort of buggered off.'
'What!'
'Long story, tell you when you get back.'
'In other words you're still hunting down the right words for the inquisition?'
'Got it in one. You writers are quite clever aren't you? So what did you want?'
'The lady I met last night said that she thought drugs were used to dope the victims and that her boyfriend was found with some of the drug on him. I've got all the details relating to dates, names etc. Interested?'
'Very. Any chance you can fax it over? I'll give Tyneside CID a call.'
'Already done, should be on your desk.'
'Good girl.' Tavistock heard him fumbling around in what sounded like a veritable sea of paper. Eventually he stopped and there was silence.
'You still there?'
'Yes, Bob, any good?'
'Could be; at least we know what he used to use. According to the lab, Caroline was given some sort of natural drug akin to something called Droperidol. Produces a state of mental detachment and indifference to the environment, yet permits communication when required. Used as a pre-med but not suitable for severely depressed patients. Or at least that's what it says here.'
'Oh, I wonder, does it mention why?'
'Nope.'

MIST

'Only this girl's brother committed suicide and she can't understand why, even after all this time.'
'Would he have been depressed?'
'His sister was raped and his father was murdered and he blamed himself; oh, and then she nearly died, the sister that is, giving birth to said rapist's daughter.'
'Yes, well I guess that would make anyone feel like jumping off a bridge. He could, of course, have been helped. I mean, let's just suppose he's depressed, goes off to see his friend Trev.'
'Who calms him down and gives him a drink of something . . . '
'And then talks him into . . . '
'Ending it all, so he jumps from a girder?'
'Perhaps he was pushed?'
There was a long pause as they both thought of the possibilities. At last Tavistock sighed and asked, 'Bob?'
'Yes, lass.'
'Is Caroline all right?'
'She's alive, if that's what you mean. A neck which she reckons would get her a walk-on part in the Rocky Horror Show and more bruises than the average TT rider.'
'Ah.'
'Oh, and she's leaving the Force.'
'Don't blame her.'
'Nor do I. Mind you, on a lighter note she does have the undivided attention of the Island's answer to Leonardo di Caprio!'
'Pardon?'
'Young Brian Clague.'
'Good! I suppose the nightmares will stop eventually,' Tavistock said, remembering Sandra's horror stricken face.
'Well, that's where she had a lot of, er, luck. She can't remember a thing about the attack. Not the proverbial sausage.'
'How come?'
'Long story, which I shall tell you about later, as for obvious reasons, i.e. my sanity would be suspect, if I now recounted what really happened to you over this phone.'
'Our mutual friend?'

MIST

'The very same.'
'I'm coming home. Are you absolutely sure this bastard has left.'
'Positive, only...'
'Only?'
'I have a feeling he's planning a comeback.'
'Right, I'll see you tomorrow. Dinner at our place and if you get there in reasonable time you can put your favourite godson to bed.'
'Deal, only I'm not helping with the lad's homework. It was fractions last time and I still can't do 'em. And I am definitely not reading him one of them daft Poke thingy books!'
'Seven thirty, and bring a bottle, if you haven't drunk that wine cellar already.'
'Oh shit!'
'Pardon.'
'I left them in the nick in Manchester, Greg's still got them!'

Tavistock laughed and hung up. Bob sat back and rubbed his tired forehead. So now he knew where and how the apprenticeship had been achieved. Something more to go in the file. Just one more fact to try and impress the Minister and the Boss. He looked at his watch and swore loudly, fluently and with feeling. He had almost thirty seconds to make the meeting at the other end of police headquarters. Bob erupted from his office not unlike Haley's Comet, trailing bits of paper in his wake.

The Honourable Member for Sodor Central and newly appointed Minister of law and order scanned the thick wad of papers in front of him and glared at the Chief Constable over thin steel-rimmed glasses. The local press had on occasions made not particularly flattering comparisons with the 'Demon Headmaster', a television programme which should, the Chief Constable thought, have had a later time slot and not been solely available to the Island's children and shift workers. In this particular instance the Chief Constable would have welcomed the 'Headmaster' with open arms. The Hon. Member in a bad mood was something few had seen but none had forgotten. And where the hell was Bob Callow?

MIST

The door burst open and Bob entered, clutching thick, brown files of paper and computer print-outs.

'You're late,' stated the Minister.

'Sorry, Sir, last minute chat with Tyneside CID on the way over here. But I did get some new useful information from them which you might find interesting.'

'This had better be good,' said the Minister, slightly mollified.

'Sit down, Bob.' The Chief Constable began to clear a space large enough to accommodate Bob's papers. Bob deposited the files on the polished wood surface and pulled up a chair.

'I've been telling the Chief Constable here how I feel that the time is now right to ask one of those profilers over,' the Minister stated, hands clasped in front of him in a parody of prayer although the dangerously sharp grey eyes belied the religious impression.

'Again?' Bob queried, puzzled.

'Do I gather that someone has already been here?'

Eyes glinted behind steel rims and Bob shuffled uncomfortably.

'Yes, Sir, we had one over last month. He sent back a fifty page report, it must be in there somewhere.' Bob pointed in the direction of the mountain of files.

'And?'

'Basically he thought the same as the police psychologist.'

'Which was?'

'It's all in the report, Sir.' Both men glared at each other. They looked, thought the Chief Constable, like two cats fighting over the one clean fishbone.

'I think that this was during the time of the previous Minister, Bob.' Bob groaned: he'd forgotten all about the recent ministerial reshufflings. 'Perhaps, Minister, I could explain or at least summarise?' the Chief Constable asked whilst glaring at his subordinate in a way guaranteed to have him thinking long vacation and no pay. The Minister nodded and drew a notepad and pen towards him. Bob watched and wondered whether the previous Minister was enjoying his retirement in Ramsey and if there would be any other political changes before this particular case was concluded. 'If it ever is,' he thought.

MIST

'Basically we have someone who has two faces. He occupies a position of trust and is well liked and respected. He is also highly intelligent but not overambitious in his chosen profession. However, underneath he wants to control. He needs to have power over life and death but most of all he wants to ensure that his victims fear him even more than death itself and half of his pleasure is derived from watching their reactions when he lets the good mask drop. This report also states that he is obsessed with the occult, that he killed at a very early age and has continued to kill, but not randomly, since that time. That he doesn't get a kick sexually from acts of a sexual nature. It is the power of fear and pain that he reacts to. Oh and about another forty odd pages detailing probable cause, profession, family background etc, etc. Any questions?'

'Just one. Bob, you've dealt with this lunatic; does this strike you as being even close?'

Bob sighed, closing his eyes and trying to piece together all the facts without admitting the additional areas of assistance given by Mannanan or even Tavistock.

'Well, for a start he's not a lunatic. Every act has been well thought out and planned in detail with the possible exceptions of crimes committed during childhood.'

'Childhood?'

'Yes, Sir, at the age of eight he helped murder and dispose of a male neighbour. He then drowned his four-year-old brother.'

'Good God.'

'Later he killed his parents and a friend, moved to Newcastle, set up his own gang and then continued to kill to control that particular group of youngsters. After that he appears to have led a fairly respectable existence working for a bank until, that is, his return to the Island. Newcastle CID now think he may be responsible for a few unsolveds when he lived there as a Trevor Mulatto and Durham constabulary have come across similar cases while he worked there as Paul Stone, although neither force has any firm evidence or at least no firmer than the sort of stuff we have. The other area of concern that all of the police forces involved with this case have highlighted is that there are periods of time when he

MIST

completely vanishes. We believe that at these points he either reverts to an alias we still know nothing about or he may even cross the Channel and have a separate identity over there.'

'So why did he come back here, to the Island?'

'We think he wants to awaken ancient Celtic Gods.'

'Oh.' The Minister looked to the Chief Constable for confirmation and shook his head; he'd known that the case of the 'Mad Druid' was a particularly difficult one but not how difficult.

'We found a skull, amongst what the profiler terms his cache of trophies. Inside was a note written in blood by one of the victims.'

'Blood?'

'I gather she didn't have a pen on her, Sir.'

'Bob,' the Chief Constable said warningly.

'Sorry,' Bob muttered.

'Well?' The Minister, ignoring the comment, leant forward, interested.

'The note gave what we think is a date and the words Mann Fort, Queens son.'

'I gather from your tone of voice that I'm not going to be overjoyed when I hear the date.'

'No, Sir.'

'Which is?'

'July the fifth.'

'Tynwald Day! Good God, we have that Royal over!'

'Exactly.'

'But we can't cancel now. It's impossible! The Chief Minister would have a fit, to say nothing of the entire Civil Service going down with the sulks. The work that's gone into it already doesn't bear thinking about. We will just have to step up security and you and your men will have to ensure he doesn't get back on the Island. And if he does, you get hold of him before we have another incident on our hands.'

'And how do we do that? We already have our current resources stretched to the limit,' asked Bob, a distinct edge to his voice.

'I don't care, that's your job; mine is to order it done,' the Minister stated in a flat cold voice. If another murder occurred he knew instinctively that it would be his resignation that would be demanded by the other 'honourable' members of Tynwald, way before those of the Chief Constable and his articulate Detective Inspector.

The Minister got up and began packing his own collection of files into a smart black leather briefcase.

Bob stared in fascination; it was like watching Mary Poppins at work with a carpet bag. At least, he thought, we've been left the rubber plant.

After the Minister had gone, the two remaining men sat in silence. After a while the Chief Constable sighed and picked up the phone, Coffee was ordered and while waiting for it to arrive he paced the room, reminding Bob very strongly of the caged lynx at the local wildlife park.

'I'm sorry, Bob. I know you've done your best on this case but until we have this one under lock and key your job is about as safe as mine, and that,' he said, pausing for effect,' is not saying much.'

The coffee arrived and was quietly left on the table in front of Bob.

'Shall I be mother?' Bob asked, beginning to pour.

'You can be the Widow Twankey for all I care, just as long as you catch the little bastard.'

'Milk, sugar?'

'Yes and one. Have you started work on notifying the public as to the current identity of Juan Moss?'

'Yes, Sir. We have posters going up all over the place: sides of lifts in all municipal carparks, billboards, ferry terminal, the airport, clubs, pubs and hotels. The press are doing pages about him and Border TV are doing a profile as are Mersey Television and the BBC. All the schools have been advised to watch out for strangers and Customs are watching all ways in and out, even the local yacht clubs and small airfields.'

'And you still think he'll get back in, don't you.'

'Yes, Sir. Look at it this way: he's used to changing his identity, appearance, voice, the lot. We have over thirty thousand bikers over

in the next couple of weeks and I'd put money on the fact that he sneaks over as one of them and then goes to ground.'
'I see. I could try to get them to cancel this year's races or at least postpone them.'
'Do you really think either Tourism or Trade and Industry would wear that?'
'No.'
'Right, well, I'll just get back to tightening security and when that fails I'm going to fall down and pray to whoever I can think of!'
'I'll join you, if it helps.'
Slowly they sipped their coffee. They had discussed at length every aspect of the case, reread every document and they had still failed to find anything new. As Bob prepared to leave the Chief Constable sat back and stared at the light fittings.
'Bob, I know you're not going to like this but I think we need to bring another man in on this, or rather woman.'
'Oh?'
'Yes. I was talking to a friend of mine last night, doesn't matter who, let's just say he's experienced this sort of thing before. Anyway they had this woman in; she's an anthropologist and specialises in religious and occult killers, at least that's what he says. I know we had someone in before. But it was at the beginning and another thing, the first victims were unmolested. This business with young Caroline Howard and this kid in Tyneside changes a lot of things. In my book he's either reverting to his old methods or something else is going on and to be honest, I don't like the thought of either.'
'And this woman's good?'
'One of the best, based at St. Andrews University. I'll give her a ring and you can pick her up from the airport when she arrives. Take her wherever she wants to go. And Bob . . . '
'Yes.'
'Introduce her to that writer friend of yours. Between the pair of them they might come up with something. The races start very soon and we can't afford any more bad press. I'll explain to our media sharks that this is not a drugs related crime spree by Free

Manx activists, but a one-off where specific drugs are used to control the victims.'

'You don't mean to say that that's what the press have been saying?'

'Oh yes, Yesterday the *Sun* carried the banner headline: "Drugs Induced Sex Orgy by Gang Leader. Is the Isle of Man the home of the new Mafia?"'

'Bloody Norah!'

'Oh, there have been better. According to the *Mirror* the Manx Free Army are waging all-out war on tourists in conjunction with a splinter group of the IRA. Even the *Telegraph* are asking how safe is the Isle of Man. Bike Capital of the World Trembles before Drug Crazed Druid's Evil Reign of Terror, would you send your children here? Oh and there's lots more; over the last few days the press have gone overboard.'

'No wonder his Lordship was upset.'

'Exactly. Let's face it, it's not just our jobs on the line here but his too, and if you think he's bad, you should have heard the Honourable Member in charge of tourism during Chief Minister's question time. I even felt sorry for the man and believe me it was a novel feeling.'

'Right, well, I'll do my best then and I'll have every available officer out there checking all links to the Island, even the unofficial ones. In fact, I may even brave the lower reaches of Pulrose and have a word with a few old stalwarts.'

Bob left and the Chief Constable reached for the phone. He didn't like this new way of thinking that all crime was a result of an unhappy childhood together with some deep biological urge. In his opinion the Druid was all bad, had been from birth and knew exactly what he was doing but if he had to bring another profiler in he would take his old friend's advice and go for the best, and hang the expense.

Tavistock arrived home to a rapturous and grateful reception which lasted for a whole half an hour. That was the time it took to dispose of various gifts and for her to find out what had happened in the

MIST

kitchen during her absence. It was with a certain amount of relief that she read the last story, kissed the last freshly cleaned cheek and started on the dinner for Richard, Bob and Moira.

Richard opened a bottle of wine, the cork making its usual welcome popping noise. The glug of wine hitting glass and the sigh with which Richard handed the proffered offering over made her look up with a frown from the vegetables she was in the process of hacking to death.

'What's the matter?'
'Nothing.'
'Nothing?'
'It can wait. That is, until Bob arrives.'
'Oh?'
'Something I discovered while you were away.'
'You know about the milkman?'
'No, not exactly.'
'But you still love me?'
'Yes, even when you prefer to clear off for days at a time, talking complete strangers into handing over their worldly goods.'
'All £5.99 of it!'
'And I still love you.'
'Richard?'
'Yes?'
'Have there been any strangers hanging around?'
'No, should there have been?'
'Only I'd like you to have a word with the children and really lay it on thick about talking to strangers.'
'This is because of the Mad Druid and the pond, is it?' Richard looked at her thoughtfully and, seeing the oddly strained expression in her eyes, searched around for something, anything, to take her mind off murder and victims. He continued in the mundane domestic chore of polishing glasses and cleaning the worst items of dried food, in particular sticky globules of ketchup off the cork place mats. 'What was this?' he asked, peering at something orange with black congealed gritty bits.

Tavistock peered at it and shrugged. 'Baked beans or it could possibly be my father's version of curried sausage and tomato. It comes off if you use a bit of bleach and a Brillo pad.'

'Great! No wonder I couldn't sleep after the feast he offered up last night. The midgets in my tum were still scraping it off my stomach linings.'

'You know, you should really stop watching children's television.'

'Why? It's one of the few perks of looking after the children when their mother leaves them for the odd strange writer and Detective Inspector.'

'Ah!'

'That first night when you stopped over in Manchester, I rang about midnight to say goodnight but you had apparently left the hotel in the company of Uncle Bob, who, I have on good authority, rattled?' Richard began counting out knives whilst watching her from under hooded eyes.

'We, um, went to, er, see a, er...'

'The sort of thing I'd be better off not knowing about, especially the really gory details.'

'Yes.' Relieved, Tavistock began stuffing sage into chicken breasts. She was in the process of wrapping them in Parma ham when the doorbell rang. Richard moved towards the hall and turning, sighed, his face a picture of pained suffering.

'Just promise me one thing.'

'What?' asked Tavistock, looking up, her voice edged with suspicion.

Richard walked towards her and physically made her look at him. Eye contact firmly established, he said succinctly, 'No more *sheep*.'

Tavistock laughed and kissed him. 'Promise, now go let the hungry hoard in before Bob drops the wine.'

Later, over coffee and Armagnac they sat around the lounge in various stages of alcoholic droop.

Richard stirred the glowing embers of the fire and threw on some more coal. Even in what was optimistically called early summer there was still a bite in the late night air.

'Richard has something to tell us, don't you, love?' Tavistock stated.

MIST

'What?'

'You said you had found something out and would tell me later and now is later.' The grandfather clock in the corner of the room struck the half hour as all eyes swivelled in Richard's direction.

'It's probably not important but it began to worry me. It's about the first body being left in our fishpond.'

'Actually that's not a bad point but as yet we don't know why.' Bob stated looking into his almost empty glass.

'I do.'

'What!' they all shrieked unanimously, making Richard smile, taking years off his features.

'I have succeeded where the great have failed,' he said triumphantly.

'He means us,' said Bob.

'I know,' Tavistock replied, 'and if he's right that smug look will take weeks to wipe off his face.'

'I, the mere staid unimaginative accountant.' Bob and Tavistock looked at one another; it was obvious that Richard was going to thoroughly enjoy his allotted fifteen minutes of fame.

'Get on with it,' said Tavistock, hurling a cushion at him.

'I have discovered that this house was originally surrounded by farmland and that part of the garden, including the pond, was built on top of the ruins of the outhouses owned by the Skillitons and the pond is on . . . '

'The site of the old woodshed!' Bob piped up.

'Yes.'

'You clever old thing you, how did you find out?' Tavistock moved towards him, a decanter in her hand.

'You read my mind,' her husband said affectionately, holding his glass out for more brandy. 'I found some old photographs of this house when it was first built and in the background you can see a low stone wall, much lower and nearer than the one we now have and behind that, almost up against the wall, a collection of rooflines. Then when I went back to the registry I came across the deeds transferring part of the farm to the original owners of this house. Of course, when we bought this place the old wall had been knocked down, the new one had been built and the buildings had gone to make way for the landscaping, such as it is.'

'So that's why we can't find the rest of the body,' Bob mused, all braincells reawakened and alert.

'Body?' Moira asked.

'Yes, when we found the woodshed Juan Moss had used we also found a whole pile of trophies, one of which was what we believe is old Dick Skilliton's skull, but we couldn't find the rest of him and now I know why. I don't suppose he could still be there under the pond?'

'I really don't know. Would it help if he was?' Richard asked, intrigued in spite of himself.

'Not really, but it would neaten a few ends.' Bob sat back, twirling the fresh supply of amber liquor in his glass. 'Speaking of which, it would also explain the wheelbarrow.'

'Wheelbarrow?' Tavistock asked, frowning slightly.

'Yes,' Bob said, leaning back against a large brocade cushion. 'When we first tried to ascertain . . . '

'Ascertain, remember that, love, for the next book, not find out or detect but ascertain!' Richard chuckled dipping into the After Eight Mint box on the small mahogany table next to him. 'Who's been putting the empties back?' he asked as he withdrew a handful of black paper but no chocolate.

'As I was saying,' Bob glared at Richard, daring him to say anything else, 'when we first tried to work out how the murderer managed to move the body, we discovered tracks similar to that made by a wheelbarrow. So we presumed that he had killed elsewhere, stored the body in some sort of shelter and then when the coast was clear or for some reason he found it necessary to move the victim, tipped the decaying corpse, wrapped in plastic, into the barrow. Wheeled it round to your house and up to the pond. Makes sense really, I mean it's fairly quiet; he could leave his vehicle if he had one elsewhere and a wheelbarrow left at the side of the road or drive with the amount of roadworks going on then, would anybody have really noticed except to say something like, "they're not making another bloody hole, are they?"'

MIST

'And that's how Brenda got rid of her husband too! Do you think that might have had something to do with it?' Tavistock asked.

'Possibly. I reckon it was just easier that way; anyway, at least we know now why he left the body in the pond, thanks of course to old Sherlock here.'

'At least it means it had nothing to do with us. For a while back there I thought it might.' Tavistock breathed a sigh of relief and carefully removed a fresh black box of mints from under the sofa. She took three herself before passing them over to Moira.

'Do you think that where he leaves the bodies is important?' Moira asked, a new train of thought hitting her as she extracted a handful of thin black chocolate squares. 'Because if it is, perhaps his final kill will be on the top of South Barrule.'

'Why?' asked Bob.

'Because that's where Mannanan was supposed to have made his fort or home.'

'Man Fort; good grief, that's what the message meant. He's going to sacrifice a royal someone on the top of South Barrule on July the fifth.' Bob almost jumped from his seat and after kissing his wife full on the lips, much to her surprise, he raced off to the hall in search of the phone.

'Easily pleased, it's always been his problem,' Moira stated. Richard and Tavistock tried not to laugh, failed and went off into near hysterics. Bob re-entered the room to find his friends and wife almost prostrate with laughter and sighed sagely.

'You know what your problem is, don't you, you all drink too much,' he said, ducking as a motley collection of cushions were hurled inexpertly towards him.

The young acne covered police constable manning the phones at the police station in Ramsey wore an expression of complete puzzlement as he tried to understand the German on the other end of the line. It wasn't so much the accent, he'd done German up at the college, it was the conversation itself.

'It ran out in front of your bike?... And you're sure it was a wolf... You did say wolf... yes, Sir, W-O-L-F... The thing is we don't have any on the Island... But the wildlife park don't have any either... Look, we had those wallabies escape and they did catch the otter, eventually, but they don't have any wolves... Look, if they had and it escaped I wouldn't be talking to you, I'd be out there catching it!... No... No... Perhaps it was a big dog? We have a lot of them, the Police dogs are really big and they look like wolves; well, they do in the dark... There is a lady over here who breeds huskies, I'll ring and see if one's gone missing. Yes, Sir... and the same to you, Sir; enjoy the rest of your holiday.' The line went dead and the young constable sighed heavily. His Sergeant, entering at that moment with a mug of tea, raised an enquiring eyebrow.

'Some German biker, Sir, said he saw a wolf tonight and it ran in front of his bike on that road down past the Tholty-Y-Will.'

'A wolf?'

'Yes, Sir, great big grey shaggy thing with ruddy great yellow teeth and red eyes.'

'Red?'

'That's what he said, yes, Sir.'

'Had he been to the pub first?'

'No, he was on his way there; actually sounded a bit shaken.'

'Oh. I see. Look, send a car up there and tell them to have a good look. We've had several complaints about some sort of dog worrying sheep near the reservoir. It's probably nothing but we'd never hear the end of it if we didn't do anything. Write it up word for word and send it to headquarters. Old Bob Callow wants reports of anything even slightly odd or strange, and that is certainly about as strange and odd as it gets.'

TT

Tavistock sat at St Ninian's traffic lights, surrounded on all sides by motorbikes, big 750 BMWs, smaller older machines and something that looked as if it ought to be pod racing on some far-flung planet not three inches from the front bumper. The children sat in a row at the back waving to the bikers over for the practice sessions, the week before the Tourist Trophy or TT started.

She noticed that one of the bikes appeared to be wobbling, the rather elderly rider pointing to the back of her car.

'Turn round,' she ordered, keeping half an eye on the lights. All three children turned round. They were wearing old paper Teletubby masks.

'Take them off, NOW!' she shouted, negotiating the left turn as the bike in front tried to shoot ahead and at the last moment realised that he was in the wrong lane and that the traffic hurling itself towards him wasn't going to stop. The ancient machine juddered, black smoke belched from the exhaust with a loud bang and the engine died. Several cars behind Tavistock started punching their horns. Other bikes snaked round both sides of the people carrier and, realising what the problem was, stopped. A group of sixth formers from St. Ninians High School, illicitly smoking on the corner, paused in their group discussion and, dropping schoolwork on the ground, moved to help the stricken biker. Carefully the machine was half pushed and half hauled up onto the pavement, the road was clear and Tavistock made a mental note not to shout at any more youngsters as they blithely walked across the road in front of her at lunchtime, or at least not for a bit.

Finally the lights changed again and she shot off towards Woodbourne Road: only another day and the Island's children would be off school for ten days. No more school runs; in fact she would leave the car in the drive and walk to the shops! Driving on

MIST

the Island's roads surrounded by bikes and other drivers, some of whom delighted in stopping to consult the odd roadmap without either bothering to pull over or to indicate, meant that her temper, always volatile, could at times seriously threaten the average tourist's life expectancy.

On the return trip she drove down the promenade. The sea sparkled a showy extravagance of light shimmering like fish scales. Beyond the breakwater the *Ben-my-Chree* was inching its way out to sea, the ferry newly painted and bright against grey concrete and dark rocks.

Somehow the Island seemed safe once again. Bob was however still convinced that Juan Moss would return. Tavistock sighed, hoping that he was wrong, A small part of her watched the boat pick up speed as it left the harbour behind and knew that it or the Sea Cat would return with a more deadly cargo. She shuddered and felt the flesh-creeping feeling of what her grandmother had said was someone walking over your grave. The car in front began to move again. Gaily dressed holiday makers promenaded past the newly painted Victorian hotels. Children waved from the horse tram as it missed her side impact bars by mere inches. The festival feeling was returning but even Richard, who usually only noticed things if you hit him over the head with a brick first, had remarked that this year's practice week lacked something. Tavistock manoeuvred the car around a van attempting to back into a blue and gold painted bollard as a policeman began to walk purposefully towards the van's driver. Perhaps it was the unusually strong and very evident police presence, or perhaps it was, as Bob had said, fear.

Tavistock moved another twenty yards or so towards the temporary lights at Summerhill and then stopped again as the lights ahead changed back to a fiery red.

Only yesterday some idiot from one of the Island's coach tour companies had asked if they could put her garden on their latest route. When it had turned out that the tour was that of visiting the murder sites used by the Mad Druid, Tavistock, barely keeping her temper, said no. After she had calmed down she'd rung Bob and let him know. Somebody somewhere was going to have quite a lot of

MIST

explaining to do to some very influential people and she hoped it would hurt.

Juan Moss leant against the wire mesh fence at the docks in Liverpool and waited for the incoming Sea Cat to arrive. At last he saw it, glinting silver in the soft evening light, a faint haze surrounding it. The group of German bikers he had attached himself to were standing in a bemused huddle as their respective machines, panniers bursting at the seams, were being weighed and measured by Steam Packet staff, each bike carefully driven onto a black rubberised mat. A young woman fiddled with the dials on a square metal box and after stilted conversation with another uniformed figure they began inspecting the bike's panniers whilst putting the owner through a series of questions.

Eventually the bikes were waved to one side. The young man from Hamburg that he had befriended ambled back towards him. Juan spoke fluent German, having at one time spent several years in West Berlin working for Barclays International. While over there he had acquired an East German passport in the name of Heinrich Kopfler. He had never had to use it until now, although when the wall had come down he had transferred it to a European one. He always planned for the future and now here it was.

His friend Klaus rode and handled the big 750cc BMW while he sat behind enjoying the feel and smell of newly waxed leather.

After fleeing the Isle of Man he had flown direct to Munich using an old British passport he had had made in the name of David Jones. Customs hadn't checked too closely and he had gambled on them not looking for that particular name. In Germany he had emptied his German accounts in the name of Heinrich Kopfler and had joined up with a group of bikers from Hamburg, one of whom was his new found friend Klaus. It had always surprised him that the authorities in East Germany had never enquired any further into the body found ten years before, under rubbish in a stairwell backing onto the wall. The old abandoned multi storey had been notorious in its day.

Perhaps the fact that sex had occurred before death and that the

MIST

emaciated remains were covered with a fine trail of bruised puncture marks had meant a low priority investigation. Juan would never know, but the victim's passport had never been enquired after and now it was worth its weight in gold.

They finally began to board, cars and vans driving in first and then the bikes: huge machines gleaming with chrome and freshly washed paint, a kaleidoscope of colours and makes. Amongst the new, a scattering of old classics could be found: Nortons and Harleys fighting for attention amidst the young pretenders.

The bikers slowly made their way up the winding green metal stairwells to the seats upstairs. Space was at a premium and they piled in, herded like cattle by smart young men and woman in blue and red uniforms, their smiles uniformly fixed. They found seats next to the window and as soon as the Sea Cat started to move slowly away from the dockside, its wake a plume of white and green water, Karl, the leader of their group, took orders for beer and sandwiches. He returned some time later with a tray of large clear plastic beakers filled with a warm brown froth. The sandwiches were a motley selection of packages. Apologising for the delay he said that things were beginning to run out so he had bought a few extra. They chattered away to the other riders around them, even to a group of schoolchildren returning from an outing and anxious to practise their hesitant German.

Juan could feel the bright festival spirit as it washed around them. He crossed his arms after finishing his beer and tuna sandwich and closed his eyes. He would soon be home and the search for his final sacrifice would be started.

They arrived at midnight, Douglas Bay lit by thousands of lights. Someone had once said in some magazine that Douglas looked like a cemetery with the lights left on. There had been a terrible row between the local and the English papers. Juan stared around him at the crowds of people milling around or simply sitting on walls and pavements watching the ferry disgorge its load: cemetery, no, or at least not yet.

The hotel they had booked into sat on a hill behind the promenade, Bikes stood side by side like bright dominoes, jostling

MIST

for space. They managed to find a parking space further up the hill, and finally made it back to the hotel to check in, bathe and sleep.

A bright morning greeted them together with the raucous shriek of gulls, scavenging for scraps left behind in discarded chip papers and polystyrene squares. Juan heard the road sweeper pass his open window and stretched. The first race would start at ten and that would give him plenty of time to breakfast and visit the library. He had started his hunt several years ago but he just needed confirmation of a few facts and dates and the stalking could begin. Happiness filled him. At last he would have what he deserved: absolute power. The power of kings and gods, the power of life and of death.

Later he sat on a wall overlooking the roundabouts at the Quarterbridge. He noticed the police were very much in evidence and in the town, posters of his old self hung everywhere. He looked at the reflection of his bald head in the bottom of his pint glass and smiled. There was no resemblance whatsoever between the bald, portly, bearded German and the slim brown haired man he had been.

The race had started almost on time and bikes tore round the course. The weather was clear and warm. Roads were dry and mist free. Already the flooded campsites were drying out and the washed out practice sessions were almost forgotten by all. People talked and roared as their favourite rider passed them by in a cloud of dust and exhaust fumes, the all-enveloping leathers a blur of colour as they passed trees and the high banked grey stone walls. Quietly, dark glasses shading his eyes, Juan leant against the barricade and watched the race. Deep inside his brain plans were being made and all contingencies thought through. Tomorrow was Mad Sunday and he would ride the TT course protected by the sheer mass and number of bikes. Half way round the second time he would request a stop and see if his prey was at home.

Sunday found him walking up a narrow leafy lane, his leather jacket slung nonchalantly over one shoulder. The house he wanted stood on the brow of a small hill, gently sleeping in the summer sunshine. A high wall surrounded it made of old stone blocks, the mortar loose and crumbly. Ivy, rich and dark veined, clambered riotously over the top. Beyond the wall he could hear the clatter of plates and the murmur of voices, interspersed with the shrill cries of excited children. A waft of barbecued steaks and sausages escaped over the wall, assailing his nostrils and causing him to salivate. He turned and made his way back down the lane. It would be easy to find and capture his next victim; in fact they hadn't even locked the gates.

Monday found him at the Grandstand on Glencrutchery road. From the stands he had a perfect view of the start line and the line of headstones in the cemetery, directly opposite. Amongst the stalls of tee-shirts, bike souvenirs and production bike hospitality tents, Tavistock Allan was signing books. He went up and bought one but something stopped him from having it signed. Instead he stood beside the brick and concrete steps and watched the small boy helping to unpack the boxes of books. He looked well fed and washed, his hair standing up at the back of his head giving him the look of a young Woody Woodpecker.

As he was staring he became aware of being watched. It was a novel and unpleasant feeling. The hairs on the nape of his neck twitched and he turned and almost ran back to his waiting companions. Bob Callow watched him go and frowned. For some reason he could almost feel a presence amongst the people surrounding Tavistock. He had no idea why he should feel this continuous unease but he did and it was getting steadily worse.

During the street party held on the road outside Summerland Juan met a local restaurant owner. The man was almost totally drunk, and staggered from table to table wishing everyone he met a wonderful holiday. Juan stuck to him like a malignant limpet and finally, when the man could hardly walk, helped him to a taxi and to his home.

The flat above the restaurant was quiet and empty; unwashed glasses stood or leant on every available surface. Dishes were piled into a grimy sink, the remains of congealed food floating on stagnant water. Juan helped the man to his bed, a rough collection

MIST

of sweat stained sheets and one heavy satin covered duvet. Afterwards he began to clean up. As the first rays of light hit the window frames he placed the last washed glass in a cupboard and closed the door. His new friend and soon to be employer would be kept sweet and sober until the fourth of July and then he would pay for his slovenliness.

On Wednesday he sat up at the bungalow watching the small child out of the corner of his eye. He had followed the boy up from Laxey on the electric tram. He had even sat behind him and his father as they passed the old mine workings and jarred and juddered their way uphill, the old Victorian brakes squealing on corners. A curtain of fine rain hung above the hills. It fell silently, not heavy enough to cancel the races but enough to ensure that each spectator was chilled to the marrow as the sidecars hurtled past. Colours blurred as bright figures leant almost onto the road, booted feet only inches from the tarmac surface, centimetres away from mutilation or death. Juan found himself watching the protagonists as they turned away from the TT Museum under the footbridge and away up the hill, the smell of hot oil and exhausts hanging in the air, the almost gladiatorial pursuit of glory exciting even him. The child watched, lips parted and hair lankly glistening in the weak sunshine. As the leaders pulled away on the final lap, the bright blue and yellow helicopter that had hovered over them dipped and whirred off across the heather clad mountains, the cameraman who had been seen precariously hanging by a strap to capture that elusive shot disappearing from view. His antics had at times impressed the crowd even more than the fast moving production machines.

The boy reluctantly waited in line for the next tram, his father obviously relieved to be going back to the relative warmth of the old wooden carriage. Juan turned and walked towards the footbridge. It wouldn't do to be spotted too many times near the boy. Once or twice the father had turned uneasily in his direction, almost as if he felt the steadily growing threat. If he became too anxious steps might be taken to send the child away again and that would never do.

MIST

The rest of TT fortnight was spent with his German friends. They drank dark, almost black, beer down on the quay in the blue and white Busheys tent. They ate pizza or chips whilst watching the various street artists. A crane hung over the promenade; a motley crowd of tourists and locals stood underneath and egged on the drunken men and women who allowed themselves to be thrown to the ground on a length of elastic. Juan frowned slightly as he passed the excited crowds of onlookers. It was sometimes incredible what people would allow themselves to do with a little persuasion from their friends. When he had the power he would make them do a lot more.

On the Saturday after the last race he returned to the ferry terminal. His ticket given up, he boarded with the other Germans in his party. Feigning sudden stomach cramps he left them and after walking round the side of the bar he found the gangplank and left the ship. So many people still milled around that he managed to merge with the crowd and find the toilets. He stayed there until he heard the muffled announcement that the *Ben-my-Chree* had docked and as soon as footsteps sounded outside, moving back towards the main terminal building, he emerged and wandered out, moving slowly with the islanders returning from their two week self imposed exile.

Martie, his new employer, grunted at him as he opened the kitchen door and putting on the proffered apron, Juan went to work, stacking dirty dishes and emptying the row of white industrial dishwashers.

Juan left for his dingy attic room at two in the morning, his eyes grit tired, muscles aching. He only had a matter of weeks to go and then this would be behind him. Slowly he crawled between worn cotton sheets and slept even before his head hit the pillow.

MIST

4th July

Richard stared out of the kitchen window and frowned. He wished that George could find a game that didn't involve water and earth. It invariably meant that he produced enough mud to completely wall the average African hut and he wasn't convinced that the hot water system could cope with the amount of steam needed for the inevitable cleaning up session. Tavistock was meeting her mother for lunch and he had been left in charge. Recently he had felt a growing unease about letting the children play outside and turning, he said as much to Bob. Bob sat at his customary place at the kitchen table, mug firmly held and cooling gently.

'You had these feelings long?' Bob asked. He had known Richard almost as long as Tavistock and it wasn't like him to imagine anything; in fact one of his more infuriating qualities was that Richard Allan had absolutely no imagination at all.

'No, not really. Only, ever since the TT started I've had this awful feeling of being watched.' Bob thought silently of Mannanan and then disregarded it.

'It's this Druid thing, everyone's uneasy. Tavistock's convinced he's come back, God knows how; perhaps she's making you uneasy by association?'

'Perhaps.'

'Did you know that I'm going to be on duty guarding our Royal tomorrow?'

'Nope, is that good, then?'

'Well, it either means that them upstairs have faith in my ability again or that the Roundheads have won. Take your pick really. What is that child doing?'

Bob moved to the back door, opened it and bellowed.

MIST

'George, you put that cat down, *now.*'

'Yes, Uncle Bob.' George sighed and frowned, his six-year-old soul hurt. He wouldn't really have thrown the cat in; well, not in the really deep bit. Grown ups were a pain. Shrugging stubby shoulders he turned and moved away to his favourite bit of shrubbery where they wouldn't be able to see him at all.

'Now where's he off to?' Bob asked, plainly exasperated.

'To eat worms,' Richard replied, filling the kettle and switching it on.

'Funny to think that hundreds of years ago that grime covered urchin could have been a prince.'

Bob looked up; suddenly someone, somewhere had walked on his grave and he didn't like the feeling at all. 'Say that again.'

'Back in 1268 one of the daughters of the ancient Kings of Mann, Godred Mac Mara, married a Scotsman, Magnus McAllistair, an officer employed by the then King of Scotland, Alexander. They eloped owing to the growing differences of opinion between the two kings which culminated in the defeat and death of Godron in 1275. Later they moved to England during the reign of Edward III, and finally their descendants returned to the Island during the Victorian heyday as the owners of one or two large hotels. So you see, if they had stayed and the Manx people had fought back at the time and, more importantly, won, George could be a prince! A horrible thought, I grant you.'

Bob almost leapt out of his chair and raced to the window just as Tavistock's car drew up outside.

'Bob, what's wrong? It's all supposition, I mean we only found out when some American was trying to prove that Wallis Simpson was related to the ancient Kings of Man and Mother got the bit between her teeth and dug out all the old archives and rattled a few skeletons she most definitely shouldn't have. Bob!'

But Bob was gone, a faint blur as he rushed headlong down the garden towards the shrubbery. Tavistock watched him surge past like a brown balding tidal wave and turned towards her husband who stood in the shade of the doorway still clutching the kettle.

'Richard?'

'I don't know, so don't ask.'

After what seemed like hours but was mere minutes Bob returned, grim faced.

'Bob?' Tavistock asked. Something in her heart began to sink slowly, a feeling of darkness bearing down.

'He's not there, and I can't see him anywhere else either but I did find this hanging from a low branch up against the wall.'

Carefully he unfolded his fist. A small gleaming circle of silver gleamed and caught the light, the intricate arrangement of strands polished like small fishy mirrors.

Tavistock reached out and touched the talisman. As she did she saw Juan Moss in front of her. He laughed out loud and in his arms he held her son.

'George,' she cried. 'He's got George.'

'Who?' Richard asked, panic surging within his throat.

'Juan Moss. The Mad Druid, he's got George.'

'Right well, before we ring the police I'm going to check every inch of this garden. Don't move.'

Richard almost lurched across the grass. 'George,' he shouted, 'George, you come out from wherever you are right now or Daddy will give you something to sulk about.'

Bob stood, eyes narrowed against the glare of the sun already beginning its daily descent, and called for backup, the mobile heavy in his hands.

Tavistock stared out across the lawn, her thoughts a mess of emotions: anger at George for being caught, despair lest he should not be found and a bitter hate which grew stronger as each minute ticked slowly by.

'He's got George,' a voice said beside them.

'We know,' acknowledged both Bob and Tavistock.

'Well, do something about it,' Mannanan shouted, suddenly losing his temper.

'And how the hell do we do that? We don't know where he's gone,' Tavistock cried, hot tears flooding her eyes.

'Well, I do and if we don't get there before him, George will be the last and final sacrifice.'

'Richard!' Tavistock shouted, 'we know where George is being taken.' Richard emerged from the bushes and brushing leaves from his face, ran back towards them.

'Where?' he asked breathlessly, hands on hips, as the stitch growing in his side became worse.

'Damn,' Bob swore. His mobile pinged at him and then bleeped irascibly.

'The bloody thing's run out.' Furiously Bob switched it off.

'He's gone to the top of South Barrule,' Mannanan stated, watching them.

'Mans Fort, of course,' Bob breathed, and then turned to Richard who had pain etched in each facial line. 'I'll take Tavistock in my car, you ring headquarters. Get hold of Brian Clague and tell him the little bastard is on his way to the old Iron Age fort on top of South Barrule. Tell him to get there a.s.a.p. but not to call out the helicopter. If he even suspects we know he may kill the child there and then. Right, Tavistock, move. Richard, the phone *now*.' So saying Bob raced to his car, pulling Tavistock with him. He pushed her unceremoniously into the back and with tyres squealing raced off down the drive, gravel spitting into the grass verge.

Mannanan sat in the passenger seat, his face grave.

'I saw him a couple of hours ago. He was up there making preparations.'

'Such as?' Bob asked, taking the next corner at speed and on the wrong side. Horns blared as he raced across the junction, narrowly missing a Ramsey bakery van.

'Sharpening a knife, and filling a cauldron with blood.'

'Oh God,' Tavistock moaned, white faced.

'Whose blood?' Bob asked. The speedometer wobbled on ninety.

'Martie Kinski, a local chef. He's thrown the body down a mine shaft at the old tin workings, the ones above the round table. That's how I knew he was back, because he'd just killed and the mask had slipped. I would have got here sooner but I wanted to find the body. The spirit stays around for a bit after death and I thought it might help if you had an identity. I guess now is not the best time to discuss it?'

MIST

'No,' Tavistock said, her voice hardly audible. 'It isn't.'

'Shit. We are never going to make it in time. Can't you do something, slow him down, anything!' Bob shouted to Mannanan who sat grimly holding onto the door handle. Desperately Bob skidded round a corner. The cyclist in front leapt into a ditch closely followed by the others in the bunch which had been straddled three abreast across the road. Alerted by the scream of brakes and roar of an engine being brutally crashed up and down gears, they had taken avoiding action just in time.

'I'll send down the mist. I can slow him up. Even druids can't race through thick fog. Then when he gets there I'll move the path, make him walk along the old track around the hill, not up it. I'll move the mist aside for you until you catch up. Get to the stile and then walk straight up towards the summit. There is a cross welded to the rock. Reach it before he does and we have a chance. Many years ago I made a pact with someone and now it's time she kept to her side of the bargain.'

Mannanan moved up through the roof and as he left the air up ahead shimmered.

Slowly the thick white fog rolled down from the top of South Barrule covering every leaf and every bog and moss covered inch.

Bob weaved his way through traffic, causing four minor accidents and a spate of complaints to police headquarters. With every nerve tingling he drove towards the southern hills. He had never before believed that he could take another life until now.

Juan fought the mist ahead. 'Where the hell has this come from?' he thought. The car slowed as he tried to remember the curve and slope of road ahead. Visibility was down to a few yards and the world outside had stopped, the sound of traffic silenced by the thick grey air. He parked an hour later and, checking that there was no-one about, dragged the small still body from the boot. The child had fought back, scraping skin with muddy fingernails; the dirt-filled welts throbbed against his cheek. From a pocket of his coat he pulled a silver flask and, tipping the boy's head back, forced the contents down his throat. George coughed and choked, spittle

MIST

erupting from his mouth. Hate and fear blazed from eyes baby large and petrified, the eyes of a rabbit caught in the oncoming glare of headlights.

Roughly pushing him ahead, Juan forced him to cross the stile and move towards the summit. Around him the earth appeared in patches. He couldn't remember the path having so many rocks in its surface and the ruts appeared wetter and boggier than they had that morning.

It seemed to him that he had walked miles and then he saw the cross ahead and, standing by it, two figures swathed by mist. They stood still, as if carved from stone. The boy at his side whimpered for his mother and again Juan struck him a glancing blow, hard enough to cause pain but not enough to damage. One of the figures made a sudden movement towards him but was checked by the other. Juan pushed the boy to one side as he squinted into the shifting wet grey curtain. George sobbed; he was tired and cold and he wanted his mother more than anybody in the world, the ache inside him a physical hurt. Something touched his hand and he looked up into eyes large and brown.

'Trust me,' said a voice. George nodded, a child's faith in magic still part of his soul.

Juan shivered, all senses heightened with the slow realisation that something was wrong. Quickly he turned back from trying to pick out the cross and regain his bearings. He already knew that somehow he must have been walking around South Barrule rather than up towards the summit. A strong sense of foreboding, heightened in part by the sudden weather change, nagged at the corners of his mind. Try as he might he couldn't shake off the growing apprehension that all was not going as planned. He looked down and screamed in rage as he realised that he was holding onto chards of heavy wet air and that the child had gone. In a fury he lurched back towards the stile and almost stumbled into a morass of mud and water, inky black and foul smelling. Beyond the pool of oozing slime the two figures stood, one of them now cradling the boy.

'Give him to me!' he screamed, his body rigid with anger.

'No,' said Tavistock, holding the child in her arms. George, terrified, clung to her as a drowning man would clutch at a rock. His small face was buried in her woollen jumper, the scent of which had calmed him but not enough to make him want to look at what was going on around him.

'He's mine!' Tavistock stroked the soft head of her only son; there was no way she was going to give her child up. Not now, not ever. She glared at Juan Moss and straightened her shoulders. Something was changing inside her. She was no longer just Tavistock Allan, the writer, mother and wife and pacifist, but the descendant of a Viking warrior and she would fight to protect her own. To the death if necessary. 'You want him, you come here and take him.' She stood on the other side of the wet bog, rage blazing in her eyes. The fear of the previous hour was gone, replaced by a cold ruthlessness. She would kill to protect her own and with the presence of Mannanan all around her she had the knowledge and the power to do it. Juan sensed that the balance had changed, the very air he breathed charged with emotion. For a moment that thought held him back but only for a moment. With the knife held high above his head he leapt the dimly bubbling ditch and moved towards Tavistock so fast she was almost taken unawares. Some sixth sense however intervened and both she and George side-stepped the flying figure. Bob, standing beside her, moved backwards as if pulled by an invisible hand.

Juan saw all this in a blur as he rushed towards them and at the same time he felt himself pushed back towards the rock strewn path. Stumbling, he turned to face them. He swore and still wielding the knife, bared yellow, nicotine stained teeth and advanced slowly towards Tavistock and the cowering child.

Bob bent down and, finding what he needed, laughed triumphantly. He had at some youthful stage been a more than averagely talented shot putter. All the old skills came back to him as he weighed the stone in his hand. Using all his strength and experience he threw the round of hardened slate and quartz strongly and accurately, hitting Juan in the face and causing him to stagger back.

MIST

'You don't understand, I need him; I need him to wake the God Mannanan,' Juan shouted at them as he raised himself from the ground, blood dripping from a long gash under his right eye.

'It's you that doesn't understand,' said a voice behind him.

Juan turned. The figure of Mannanan Mac Lir stood directly behind him. Around them the peat and heather bent low as if being pushed down by the weight of the slowly solidifying air. Mannanan stood taller, or so it seemed to Tavistock and Bob, and his voice had changed; it was thicker, colder and stronger. His face too had altered; any vestige of humanity had been washed from it, leaving a mask the colour of grey agate.

'My Lord.' Juan fell on his knees before the tall robed figure. 'I woke you, and now you must allow me to have the power of the earth and stone, sea and sky as it is written in the old runic letters. You must obey *me*.' Juan's voice rose triumphantly and he beat the earth with his fists.

'You really have no idea, do you, boy?' Mannanan said, his voice almost a sneer. He leant over the figure prostrated before him, his shadow falling over the knife that Juan still held. Soundlessly Mannanan knelt down in front of him. Juan felt his head forced up until he had to look into Mannanan's eyes, now level with his own.

'You see, boy, you didn't wake me because I was never asleep; you woke Her.'

Juan heard the soft breath behind him and suddenly, for the first time in his life, fear gripped him. He turned and saw rising from the earth the figure of a wolf. Its fur was matted rust red and its breath stank of decay and rotting flesh. The eyes, yellow with pinpoints of black, rested on him for a moment and then it raised its head and howled.

The sound stunned the watchers. Tavistock clasped George to her, brave no longer. Bob felt himself rooted to the spot, unable to move or speak.

As the last wave of noise receded, swallowed up by the surrounding fog, now thicker and greener than before, the wolf began to change. Its face fattened and the eyes grew ever more human. Lips parted and hair snaked to the ground a rich deep brown.

MIST

'Why have you summoned me,' the figure asked, looking straight at Mannanan.

Juan, suddenly piqued by the very fact that he was being ignored by both Spirits, stood up and waved his knife in the air.

'He didn't, I did!' he shouted.

'But you are a boy, a child, a mere nothing. And I am Baal. How could you have obtained the knowledge to do this?' Baal asked, moving towards him. Her long dress of green skimmed over the surface of the ground, like the skin of a large snake.

'I spilled the blood and sang the old forgotten songs; I woke the earth,' Juan stated proudly. The woman in front of him was more beautiful than he had ever imagined anyone could be, her face, the face of a Roman or Greek statue, marble white.

'And what do you want?' she asked, her voice suddenly warm and honeyed.

'I want the power. I want what you have.'

'Then come to me and take it,' she whispered, opening her arms wide as if to embrace a lover or child. Juan made a movement towards her but she had suddenly turned towards Mannanan. Her voice changed; the pitch lowered. 'Unless he objects? Do you, old one? Or will you still protect those who have been birthed upon your puny square of land?' Baal glared across the path at Mannanan, as if daring him to speak. Mannanan shrugged, his face blank, devoid of feeling.

'Take him by all means. He has forfeited any right to my protection long ago when he killed his own.'

'Indeed. Then perhaps we do have a common interest.' Baal moved towards Juan and as she did something inside his mind rebelled. This was not as he had imagined. No fire flashes or rolls of thunder. The power he felt around him belonged not to him but to the two entities either side.

'You want power, then come and touch it.' Baal smiled at him. The smile was terrible and as he looked into the black pupils of her eyes he thought he saw his future, swallowed up as if by a black hole whirling helplessly towards infinity.

'No!' he screamed and turning towards the two figures of Bob and

Tavistock, implored them with eyes bright with fear to do something. They said nothing and remained motionless, watching, both powerless to intervene.

'Come to me.' Baal began to grow, spreading within the misty air, potent and amoral; neither good or evil. The very air crackled with energy.

'Come. You will be the last sacrifice, as was written. So shall it end.' On the word 'come', the ground beneath Juan began to dissolve. Bog formed beneath him, turning solid earth to mud and then to dank, gas filled marsh. Slowly he began to sink into the mire. Dribbling saliva, he clutched desperately at the hem of Mannanan's gown. He clawed at the fabric, his brain suddenly filled with horrors as he felt himself being sucked down, the liquid beneath him bottomless. Around him bone fragments began to rise to the surface. One, a sheep's skull, banged against his leg causing him to look into the festering ooze and looking back up at him through the water, he saw the face of his brother. The face looked at him and smiled back, the teeth drawn back in a parody of the wolf's.

Mannanan looked down on him and twitched the soft cloth away from his grasp. 'You wanted this! You worked towards it. This is what you did to the people who served you, so now serve your mistress, boy.'

Baal moved towards the sinking form, covering him with her body. Juan screamed, the scream echoing as the howl had echoed. Desperately he tried to pull himself up out of the cloying earth. His knife flashed as he tried to cut at the figure around him and at the skeletal hands pulling him deeper into the bog, its consistency now that of thick porridge.

Bob, suddenly able to move, found himself running towards the desperately struggling man and realised with a shock that Juan was cutting himself in the struggle, like a wild animal caught in a trap. 'Nobody deserves to die like that, not even him,' he thought. Juan began to scream hysterically, the words muffled and unintelligible. With one last thrust of the silver knife, now heavily bloodstained, he tried to cut Baal's throat but found the knife caught in strong

MIST

hands. Slowly the blade was turned and held against his own throat. He looked up into eyes which mirrored his own and began to beg, whimpering with fear. 'Mercy, please have mercy,' he whispered. Baal bent and kissed him. Juan cringed, relief apparent on his face, and then without any warning Baal brought the blade down in an arc and slashed his throat. Blood spurted from severed arteries and sprayed the horrified onlookers. The figure crumpled like an old rag doll and fell back, swallowed up and then covered completely by an oily film of brackish water. Silence filled the surrounding area as Bob, Tavistock and Mannanan stood and looked down into the quietly bubbling grave of Juan Moss. A black beetle, glossy and fat, skittered across the surface and disappeared into a tuft of grass.

The mist began to lift, the last golden rays of sunshine striking the cross and surrounding heather in a sudden blaze of warmth. The sound of many running feet and the steel clang of slamming car doors reached them. Brian and Richard were the first to arrive, both breathless from their headlong rush uphill.

'Sir, was that . . . ?' Brian asked, pointing at the still water.

'Yes, yes it was,' Bob said, reaction beginning to set in.

'What a horrible way to go.'

'Yes, yes, it was.' For some reason Bob could almost feel pity towards the dead man.

'We could see him, you know, shouting and waving that great knife around,' another Police Constable said.

'Nothing you could do, Bob. I saw it all. Well, at least we're all saved the trouble of a trial.' The deep tones of the Chief Constable reached Bob as he began to move back towards Tavistock and the small still figure of George.

'Funny, really, how they all seem to kill themselves in the end. Perhaps it's the guilt. That profiler said more or less the same, didn't she?'

Bob nodded, still stunned, willing to agree to anything. Blood lay sticky against his skin, the smell that of warm meat. Without warning his throat felt hot with the tang of bile rising. He turned and threw up into a ditch. His chief stood behind him, shielding

MIST

him from his men, and when he had finished handed him a large cotton handkerchief.

'Thanks,' he muttered.

'Take your time, Bob, just take your time.'

Richard arrived, breathing hard, and carefully taking his son in strong arms, thanked Bob with his eyes before moving back down towards the waiting cars, their metal sides glinting in the evening light. Tavistock walked with him, thankful for her husband's quiet strength and lack of questions.

Uniformed officers appeared in ever increasing numbers as the word spread and the clear-up began. They found the blood filled cauldron first, then the runes and an old book of legends which had once been Morag's. One of the pages was loose and as the police constable went to pick it up it fluttered off. Caught by a sudden gust of wind the page lifted and blew away across red tinged grass and heather. The page contained the solitary picture of an old man leaning on a staff.

After they had gone and the moon shone silver across the barren landscape, the lone figures of a man and a large four legged animal could be seen silhouetted against the blue-black night sky. After a time the man turned and began to walk back down the footpath towards the road below. The animal remained poised above the steep sides; it howled once into the honey scented night air before launching itself upwards and into the star studded void, where it disappeared into a wisp of fine cloud, hurriedly moving across the silver face of the low hanging moon.

Later they all crowded round the small figure of George who sat up in his parents' bed surrounded by pillows and pieces of Lego. He was eating chicken soup, glad to be home and the centre of attention but puzzled as to the reason.

His father ruffled his hair and sighed. Richard still couldn't understand how George had managed to survive but he had and he rather thought that questioning either Bob or his wife would be futile.

The phone rang downstairs, its sound cutting the peaceful silence.

MIST

'I'll get it.' Richard said, exiting. Bob and Tavistock turned to the figure on the bed. Mannanan had promised he would remember nothing but they wanted to check. Quietly Bob moved to the door and listened. Tavistock took her son's hand and stroked it, trying to form the right words.

'Mum?' George asked, staring past her.

'Yes, my love.'

'Who's that man?'

'Which man?'

'The one by the door.'

Tavistock, suddenly worried, looked towards Bob, who shrugged. Perhaps he'd forgotten more than they'd bargained for. 'That's Uncle Bob. Your godfather, remember. You go to football with him.'

'Oh, I know that. No, I mean the other one. The one Daddy just walked through.'

'What!' Both Bob and Tavistock turned on Mannanan who, ignoring them, went to stand at the foot of the bed.

'I am Mannanan Mac Lir, Navigator, Magician and protector of the Isle of your birth.'

'Are you dead?' asked George, interested.

'Not exactly.'

Tavistock moved towards Mannanan, the look on her face boding no good for anyone, even dead ones.

'You see,' Mannanan said, 'I am only visible to a very few including your mother and your Uncle Bob; oh, and now you, of course.'

'And you saved me from the nasty man?'

'Well, yes.' They all looked anxiously at the figure in the bed. Would the horror of the previous night be reawakened? George sat back, a strangely beatific smile on his round face.

'Cool!' he said. 'Mum?'

'Yes?'

'Can I take him to school tomorrow?'

'No!' Tavistock, Bob and Mannanan said, their combined tone of voice full, final and with no possible chance of appeal.

Acknowledgements

With many thanks to:
The Office of the Chief Constable and the Isle of Man Constabulary
Manx Airlines
The Isle of Man Steam Packet Co Limited
Various members of Tynwald who wish to remain anonymous
David Ashworth of the Lexicon Bookshop for his advice
All those at the Pentland Press
And finally, all my friends and relatives who had to put up with my mood swings and oddball conversations